Monsters

Brad D. Sibbersen

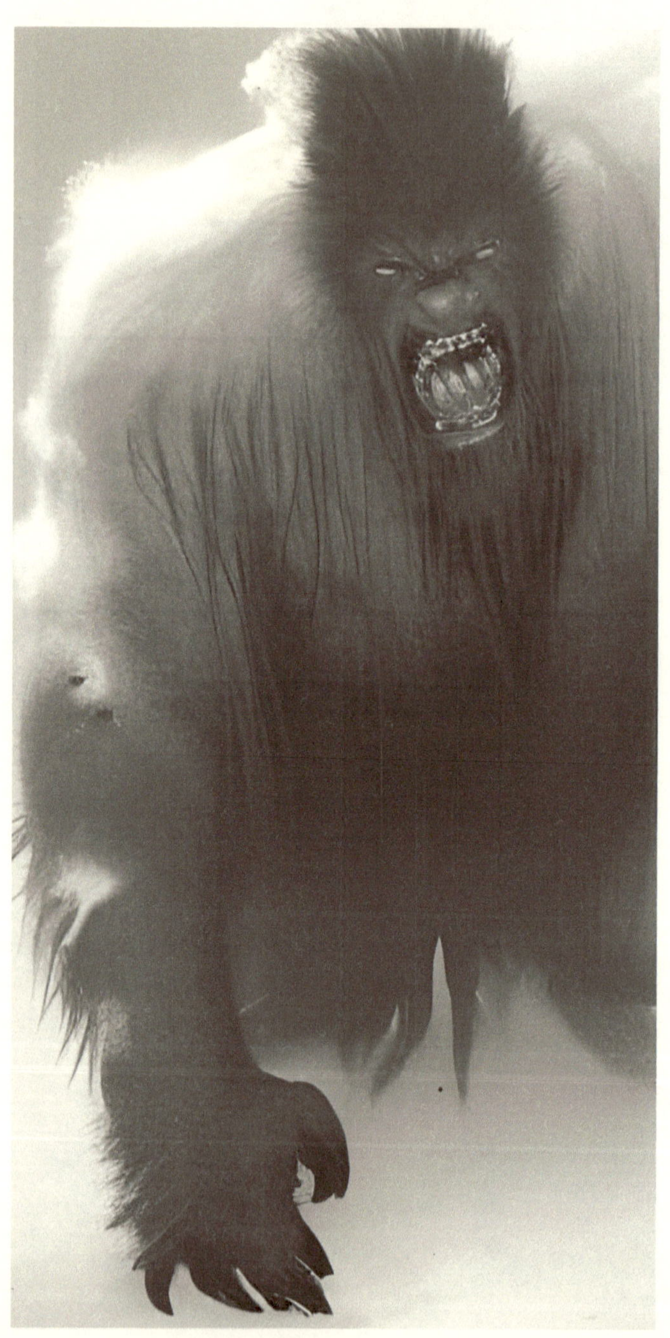

Quality books, bizarre titles, available wherever books are sold!

BOMBED. It was the easiest gig imaginable – break into a forgotten Cold War era laboratory and steal a discredited experimental device. But no one told Dac Wheeler that the device in question was a super bomb, and that after all these years it was still armed.

DEMONS AND DRAGONS. The Black Game. The most infamous tabletop game of them all. At the height of the fantasy roleplaying boom, it was banned, nationwide, after the mysterious deaths of several players. Was it all just an urban legend, another case of 1980s satanic panic, or is there something wrong with The Black Game? Something evil?

THE FAERIE PIT. Deep in the forest primeval it slumbers. Invisible. Benign. Until you awaken it. Then it will make all your dreams come true. There's only one catch. Once aroused, it's always hungry. And it feeds on blood.

AMITYVILLE SUBDIVISION. A person can haunt a house, but can a house haunt a person? Steven Madoff wouldn't have thought so, but after fleeing one of the most haunted houses in America he spent the next several years erecting an altar to it - seven identical homes, an entire subdivision of evil.

WELCOME TO MAD SCIENCE U. All that junk science you see in old movies? It's real. But it's only taught in one place - the Madiport Island University of Science and Technology, an ultra top-secret learning facility located in the heart of the infamous Bermuda Triangle. So what is Kevin Landon, perennial C+ student, doing here?

LOOK WHAT'S HAPPENED TO MAD SCIENCE U. In this epic sequel to Welcome to Mad Science U, displaced normie Kevin Landon and his hyper-brilliant classmates are compelled to violate the laws of time itself to save one of their own. But when their time machine is irreversibly damaged and will only travel further into the past, how will they ever get home again???

NIGHT OF THE HORNÉD GOD. There's an alternate universe right beneath our feet, a universe of basements and sub-basements, steam tunnels, catacombs, subways and sewers. And it's inhabited. By the homeless, the forgotten, the disenfranchised. And something else. Something evil, called up from the furthest reaches of Hell to prey on the living and the dead alike on the Night of the Hornéd God.

DEADBURBIA. Kim and her friends thought they were in trouble when they had a run-in with some kids from the wrong side of the tracks, but nothing could have prepared any of them for the horror that was to follow in this tale of undead madness that begins with an epilogue and ends when six innocent souls are utterly consumed by the Deadburbia.

PULP: is published by Inept Concepts
Vol. 1, No. 1, October, 2023 issue

This issue:

She haunts the fringes of civilization, tragically beautiful and forever alone, her only solace the knowledge that she is

The Master of Frankenstein

1

The first thing she remembered was the last thing she'd remembered; pain and humiliation, and fear.

No, that wasn't right.

The first thing she remembered was a strange haze, swimming through it, as if visually attempting to come up for air. And then *his* kindly, handsome, intelligent face, filling the world, smiling down upon her with a mixture of emotions she only later came to identify and understand: relief and satisfaction, and joy. Her doctor.

Doctor Emrys Frankenstein.

Even as he lifted her off the still-smoking table the storm outside seemed to diminish, as if, having done its duty, it knew it was no longer needed. The rain slackened off and the thunder rumbled away to parts unknown, leaving only the lightning, which flickered silently against the harsh stone walls of the laboratory.

"Igor! Fetch me that blanket so as to cover her shame!" And the stitches, though he didn't say this part aloud.

"My name," the dwarf reminded him, "is Pernicus."

"I've taken the first step in supplanting God Himself," Emrys reminded the little man. "Won't you allow me this one indulgence?"

"I will not," Pernicus assured him.

For her part the patchwork girl was silent, her reaction to these men that of a feral animal, though one so fearful and discombobulated that she could only stare at them in muddled confusion. She didn't struggle as Emrys wrapped her loosely in the mauve blanket and steadied her with a single arm around her shoulders.

"Where?" Pernicus asked, leading the way.

"The chamber across from my own. I've cleared the apartment of all but necessities, and specially prepared the bed."

The special preparations Dr. Frankenstein was referring to were manacled chains, which he secured around his unprotesting creation's narrow wrists. Still wrapped in the mauve blanket, she collapsed into the fourposter bed as if their slow descent down the two lengths of stairs had utterly exhausted her. Emrys pressed the stethoscope he carried against her cool, white chest, listened, nodded with detached satisfaction. He checked her pulse at her throat, prompting her to wince, then smiled and ran a gentle hand through her longish blonde hair to pacify her.

"It's all right," he whispered, as if speaking to a child. "Everything is going to be all right now."

She only stared, her eyes wide, emphasizing the disparity in size and color between the pair. Emrys frowned. A glaring imperfection, but it couldn't have been helped.

"You'll sleep now," he told her. "Tomorrow, your new life truly begins."

She said nothing, of course, but the way she stared... it was almost as if she did understand, a little.

He doused the lamp in the room and took it with him. She didn't protest or react to the sudden darkness, but he left the chamber door open and the lamps burning in the hallway, just in case. Then he retired to his own apartments, where he slept not a wink, despite having dozed but a few scant hours in the entirety of the preceding week.

That was the end of Autumn Frankenstein's first day.

2

"*Franks*...tine."

"Better, better," Emrys nodded encouragingly.

He'd set up class in the conservatory, dragging the chalkboard upstairs from his laboratory proper. Autumn, bareheaded and barefoot, wore a long-sleeved house dress, effectively hiding the jagged scars where one arm and both legs had been surgically grafted to her torso. Aside from her disproportionate eyes, and a permanent scar where, in a previous life, her upper lip had been split, forever shadowing her countenance with the merest hint of a sneer, she was quite lovely. An unusually pallid complexion and the deformed hand at the end of her mismatched right arm completed the short list of her imperfections. Her charms, conversely, were many, more then compensating, and to the eye she was nothing if not an arresting, if flawed, young beauty.

"Frank. En. Stein," Emrys repeated patiently.

"Frank. En. *Stein*."

"Wonderful!" He clapped his hands together. "That's your name! Autumn Frankenstein."

"Autumn." That particular series of sounds gave her a rush of pleasure. She liked it.

"And you *are* a Frankenstein, as much as if you

9

sprang from my own loins," Emrys assured her. "For am I not your progenitor?"

"Pro...genitor," she repeated.

"Yes! Good! No, more than good, glorious!"

She smiled, pleased to have pleased him.

Scratching the surname across the chalkboard, Emrys indicated the first latter.

Autumn scrunched up her face.

"F," she finally said.

"Now the sound F makes?" Emrys prodded.

"Ffffff," Autumn hissed, then laughed.

That laugh! He had to look away. Something clutched at his chest that he quickly dismissed.

"Yes," he told her, finding a smile. She smiled back.

"She's clearly retained an enormous amount of general knowledge from her previous life," Emrys confided in Pernicus that night. "I'm going to start her on proper reading tomorrow, I think. With any luck the basics – reading comprehension, simple mathematics, basic conceptualizations – are all still in there and just need a metaphorical kick in the seat to get her back up to speed."

"You sound quite hopeful. Doctor."

"Shouldn't I? She's calm, collected, eager to learn. I've already surpassed my great uncle's initial, clumsy achievements in every possible way." Emrys stared off into the distance, momentarily lost in his own thoughts. "Perhaps that was his mistake all along. Perhaps he should have begun with the gentler sex."

"You're still chaining her to her bed at night," Pernicus pointed out.

"Well no more. That ends tonight. I will lock her door – from the outside, of course – but at this point that is for her own protection, not ours."

"I see," Pernicus said.

That was the end of Autumn Frankenstein's first week.

3

"The Holy Bible. Goethe. Sophocles. Dante." Emrys nodded appreciably. "That's an impressive list for a twelve-week-old."

"How is it," Autumn asked, setting the leather-bound copy of *Faust* aside, "that I am whole and complete at such a young age?" She tilted her head as she waited for the answer.

"You've delved into some biology, then?" Emrys grinned.

"I have."

"Then I suppose it's time I tell you about the birds and the bees, or rather the electrophores and the beakers." He sat down on the couch next to her and took her hands in his. "My dear Autumn, you are not life as mankind has heretofore known it. You were not crafted from clay nor torn from the loin of a god, but rather created by a man, myself, almost though not quite the very first of your kind."

"A monster," Autumn said without inflection.

"No! Never! Where did you even hear that word?"

"Everywhere!" Autumn exclaimed, indicating the shelves of books lining the room. "Always that is what the *other* is referred to as! *Monster*."

"You are **not** a monster!" Emrys assured her, squeezing her hand so tightly it hurt them both. "You're a revelation! A wonder! The next step in mankind's evolution into godhood!"

"Your own books caution against this," Autumn grinned.

"Not caution! Fear! The same fear that hounded my father, and his father, to early graves! But I corrected their error. Man, the male of the species, is inherently physical and violent. Not so woman! She is loving, indulgent, motherly. *That* was their mistake, and I have corrected it, with you!"

"What am I, then?" she asked. He turned away.

"More than the sum of your parts," he said quietly.

"These scars, they suggest..."

"Yes."

"I am a monster then. Cobbled together from... the dead."

"No! Nothing so vulgar! Crafted, not cobbled! And with love! Love for life, and knowledge! The very antithesis of *dead*."

He was right, of course. And yet she wondered.

In time Autumn was given free rein to roam the castle's many rooms at her leisure, and even to explore the expansive grounds, at first with a protective, ever-alert Emrys by her side, but soon enough on her own, after promising that she would not stray out of sight of the highest tower, which would mean that she had strayed off the grounds proper. More and more she found herself dallying within the wood that surrounded the castle, reveling in the smell of pine needles and moist, rich earth. The small animals she encountered there kept their distance but watched her, curiously, from afar, and she took to carrying handfuls of nuts and bits of fruit in the hopes of coaxing a squirrel or jay or bunny rabbit closer. This never quite worked, but if she placed the treat on the ground and removed herself a fair distance, the squirrels, at least, would eventually dart in and snatch the morsel away. They were adorable, and she laughed every time. So very distracted was she by all of it that she never noticed that Pernicus was following her, watching, every single time.

One day, as she spiral-peeled the thin bark off a young deciduous tree, marveling at the sensation, there was an explosion.

She started, momentarily terrified. But curiosity got the best of her and she moved in the direction of the unexpected sound, even now recognizing the more familiar sounds of motion and a human voice. A man's voice, not entire unlike her Doctor's, but rougher and far less refined.

"Damn't t' hell!" the voice proclaimed.

Something behind her. She turned, looked around. Did the shrubbery... move? Was something following her?

No. Her imagination. She knew all about imagination. It was the seed that grew the many wonderful stories she read in Emrys' books. There was nothing there. She moved on, towards the voice.

Pernicus, hidden in the shrubbery Autumn had briefly examined, breathed a sigh of relief, but remained agitated. What should he do? What should he do??

Autumn wove her way through the trees, peering, listening.

There! It was a man!

She froze, staring, in a state not quite but almost akin to awe. Aside from Emrys, and Pernicus, she'd never laid eyes on another human being before. This one wore clothes identifying him as a common laborer, and carried a hunting rifle. *That* had been the sound she'd heard. Grousing out loud, the man was using the rifle to part the branches of a brier bush, apparently in search of something. Autumn openly stared, fascinated. What was he doing? Perhaps she could apply deductive reasoning, and figure out the mystery. Deductive reasoning was always one of her favorite lessons, and wouldn't Emrys be proud when she informed him she'd practiced it under real-life circumstances?

So. The man had a gun, and he had fired it. At what? Another man, perhaps, but more likely an animal. He was hunting then, and the animal he'd fired at had escaped his depredations and darted into the brier bushes, where he couldn't get at it, even if he did now manage to shoot it. The clever little thing! She giggled and clapped her hands at the creature's resourcefulness, and now the hunter was the one who started, turning in her direction, the shadow of guilt creeping across his face, already blathering excuses and apologies.

"And sure it is, ma'am, that I'm only just now spying the tower in the distance an' realizing I've strayed onto castle land..."

He trailed off, his eyes growing wide. His hands began to shake.

"No..." he said, staring at her. "No, an' it cannot be!"

He took a frightened step backwards, raised the gun as if to fire on her but then apparently thought better of it. Instead, he let out a scream that chilled her borrowed bones and then turned and fled, shrieking, out of the wood and across the summer-flower fields in the direction of...

(*the village*)

Yes. The village.

How did she know this?

4

"It's true then!" Autumn howled, lashing out with a balled fist. "I AM a monster!"

She struck the dining hall table with all the force and fury her unique physiognomy provided her, and the surface of it cracked, straight through. Three inches of solid oak, it was.

"Autumn! Calm yourself! You are *not* a monster!"

"His reaction was unmistakable! It was fear, and terror! And from these next comes hate, as surely as night follows day!" She buried her face in her hands then, and wept.

"Pernicus!" Emrys snapped. "Find out who this poacher was and file a complaint with the authorities! Now!"

The dwarf scampered off to do his master's bidding.

Emrys turned his attention back to Autumn, gently – though cautiously – taking her into his arms.

"You are *not* a monster," he repeated. "The man was frightened at being seen, because he was breaking the law, and knew it."

"I may be a child as you measure such things," Autumn sniffled, "but I'm am not so naive as to believe your words. I know what I saw. What I felt."

"Look!" Emrys snapped, roughly seizing her head and turning it so that she looked upon herself herself in the wall mirror. "You are beautiful! Only the tiniest of imperfections betray your scientific origins, and they are 'flaws' well within the bounds of natural probability! In perusing the library how many pictures have you chanced across purporting to depict the beauty of the female form? Hundreds? Thousands? Look! You are no different! No different! More than that – you are, I say, superior to them all!"

And then he pressed his lips to hers...instantly her fingers were running through his thick, wonderful hair...and as if guided by knowledge preordained she forced her tongue into his mouth – a cold, wet slug it was yet he did not protest but rather reciprocated, and a glorious heat grew within her as she curled one of her long legs around his own and began gyrating rhythmically against his excitement.

"Autumn... Autumn... my love..." he gasped.

They collapsed onto the carpet, a tangle of arms and legs and gasps, and did what came naturally.

Or, perhaps in this case, unnaturally.

"So you've done it, then," Pernicus frowned. "I can see it written all over your face."

"Don't dare judge me, dwarf," Emrys warned. "I love her."

"It's a sin. Repugnant."

"I answer to a higher morality."

"So you seem to believe."

"Did you solve our little... problem?" the doctor asked, changing the subject.

"The poacher's been identified and arrested. As for the heart of it, naturally the village gossips are all aflutter. Every washer woman and pub rat extant is already carefully crafting their own unique version of events, and doubtless it will end fully entrenched in local folklore. Don't think any of them properly takes it seriously though."

"We can only hope."

5

"So soon after her encounter in the woods?" Pernicus frowned. "I don't think it wise."

"I can't hide her away forever!" Emrys snapped. "Already she has so many questions. She must be properly socialized. I'll take her to Rothenburg. That's far enough away that we won't be recognized."

"You play with fire," Pernicus said.

"Prometheus played with fire, and the whole of the world was changed for the better," Emrys replied. "Now are you going to stand about, parroting cliches, or are you going to prepare the coach?"

"Fire," Pernicus repeated as he toddled off.

They traveled for the entirety of the morning and more, reaching Rothenburg in the early afternoon. At Emrys' suggestion Autumn wore a veil and makeup to mask her imperfections, and her dress hid her scars. They took rooms, dined, walked the streets arm-in-arm in the cool autumn sunlight, and even engaged in light conversation with strangers to them both, and she loved every moment of it. For his part, her Doctor, her love, was nervous and distracted, constantly on the lookout for.. something.

They watched the sunset from a small bridge spanning a rapid, negligible stream. It was glorious.

"Tell me," Autumn playfully demanded. "Tell me how you did it. How I came to be."

"The science is quite beyond your current..." he began.

"Not the science, my darling. The romance of it! The story!"

"Very well. My father's father's brother was, of course, Victor Frankenstein, he who first crafted a man from the remnants of other men. It did not end well for him, as his bitter creation, all but abandoned by his creator, turned on him and took from him everything he held dear, climaxing with his own life. That would have been the end of it, but that my father found himself compelled to follow in Uncle Victor's footsteps, setting into motion still more tragedy." Emrys sighed and Autumn took his hand, giving it what she thought was a gentle squeeze. He greatly appreciated the gesture and managed not to wince.

"And yet you took the chance, continuing their inquiries," she said. "For which I am, of course, eternally grateful."

"Only because I realized their error, their dogged insistence on breathing fresh life into a *man*." He smiled. And while it was meant to be a bemused smile it came across as somehow...haunted. "The gentler sex, that was the key. So obvious, in retrospect."

"Tell me more. How I, specifically, came to be."

He turned away, not wishing to look into her eyes.

"It's all too...morbid. Such things are not for the ears of a lady."

"Am I a lady, then? Lady Frankenstein?" She tried it on again, lingering over it this time: "Lady Frankenstein."

"I am no lord," Emrys said quietly, "but if you would deign to be *Mrs.* Emrys Frankenstein you would do me an honor I hardly hope to deserve."

"Tell me," she repeated. "Tell your newly betrothed – for of course my answer is yes – how I came to be. An...engagement present, as it were."

"Of the most gruesome sort," Emrys frowned. The sun had almost set and it was growing dark. "Very well. You are the amalgamation of the most beautiful woman I ever laid eyes upon, and those...addendum necessary to make that woman whole."

"You suppress the morbid particulars. Spare no detail. I insist."

"You possess the longest, most wonderful legs I could acquire, and – my sole regret – a single arm that was the only such available to me. I had to replace one eye, again compelled by circumstance to use that which was available. Have you not heard enough?" He was clearly uncomfortable discussing this with her.

Her eyes moved upstream, and she watched the water in silence for a time.

"Who was I, before?" she finally asked. "'The most beautiful woman you ever did lay eyes upon', you say. Who was she? Did you know her?"

"I did not know her."

"No matter," Autumn said after a time. "She is dead, and I am alive. Gloriously alive! Alive and happy and betrothed!" She took his arm, her eyes twinkling. "Kindly escort me back to my room," she requested.

6

"It will take time," his agent repeated.

"Time is the one thing I do not care to waste!" the doctor barked. "How difficult can it be to sell a castle? Even a niggling example of its ilk such as this? Doesn't every cheap, gaudy lord dream of residing in a castle of his very own?"

"It's not difficult at all, if one doesn't care what one gets for it. I'll broker a deal with the next passerby for whatever Goldmarks they have on their person, if you absolutely insist. You'll take a bath on my fees, of course..."

"Yes, yes!" Emrys dismissed the man's sarcasm with a wave.

18

"Why the great hurry, if you don't mind my asking?" the agent inquired.

"I wish to re-locate to London, posthaste. I won't be returning, and the funds would be invaluable in establishing myself there."

"Business?"

"No." A small amount of pride crept into the doctor's voice. "I'm to be married."

"Oh." The agent, who'd known Emrys both personally and professionally for some time, was somewhat taken aback. "So soon? Might I inquire...?"

"You might not. This is a professional call and I insist it remain so. How can I turn this draughty old pile of rocks into cash, quickly? That is the only thing I wish to hear from you."

"Very well. You could lease it out. I could secure you a loan against its value until it is sold, at very good rates..."

"Yes. That sounds like the best course of action. Set the wheels into motion."

The agent fussily packed up his things, shook Emrys' hand, and took his leave.

Upstairs, locked in her apartment, Autumn fretted and fumed. Why had she not been allowed to meet her fiance's friend and business associate? Of course, she could have easily forced the lock, given her unnatural strength, but she didn't want to upset Emrys. Besides, it was the *principle* of the thing which upset her, less so the specifics themselves. Was Emrys ashamed of her? She stared at her visage in the mirror for the thousandth time that day and while it was true that she was a physically flawed being, certainly it was not to the extent that he should deem it necessary to hide her away like some deformed, bastard relative. And, after all, had they not visited Rothenburg? Dined there, and walked the streets, in full public view?

She stepped to the window as she heard the coach horses clamp by, trying to catch a glimpse of their visitor. There, the horses... his driver... and... Yes! The agent's head appeared, framed by the coach window, even as he carelessly glanced back towards the castle, his eyes popping with surprise and...fright?.. as they found her. His jaw appeared to have come loose it dropped so suddenly. Ashamed and frighted, Autumn melted back into the shadows even as she heard him demand his driver stop.

The casual clop-clop of the horses ceased. She heard snippets of a rapid-fire, breathless parade of questions and clarifications: "Did you see?" "There, in the tower window!" She flattened herself against the wall next to the window, assuring that she could not be seen from below. Was she so hideous? No! Of course not! Rothenburg proved that! What, then, inspired this abject terror is someone close to Emrys? For in her short memory, he was the only individual ever to...

No. Not the only.

The poacher.

Outside, the driver finally urged his horses on again, and soon the coach was again rattling its way down the drive towards the cliff-side road.

Autumn barely noticed. Her mind was racing. A tenacious need to solve this mystery gripped her like a physical thing, and the proverbial cat that curiosity killed be nine times damned, she would have satisfaction.

7

"I want to go into the village," Autumn informed Emrys over dinner. Pernicus had prepared a quarter ham purchased just that afternoon in the very same village, garnishing it with red potatoes, broiled carrots, and served with a bottle of Marcobrunner Auslese from the castle's near-depleted cellar.

"I forbid it," Emrys replied casually over his glass of wine.

"But why?"

"My family history is such that I am... less than welcome there. This is why I'm moving us to London, where the name Frankenstein is not so well known."

"But surely nothing can come from simply walking down the street in broad daylight? Peering into the shops? Seeing what there is to see?"

"They would point. Stare. Bend their heads together and whisper. It would upset you."

"I submit to you, darling, that I am made of sterner stuff."

"I won't subject the woman I love to ridicule and gossip. The subject is closed."

No, it wasn't.

It was three days more before her chance arose.

Men were arriving in the morning, to cart off Emrys' laboratory preparatory to shipping it to England. He and Pernicus were meticulously packing each and every phial and scale and piece of equipment, engaged with the task to distraction. They'd risen with the sun and it was now after noon with the task only just begun. She prepared them a small lunch to much thanks and then retreated upstairs "to rest".

Ten minutes later she was dashing across the grounds, into the surrounding trees. At the opposite end of the wood she found herself at very nearly the furthest point of the castle drive, out of sight even from the uppermost of its battlements, and this she followed to the cliff road that wound around the opposing mountainside and down, down, into the village.

The village, she mused. She didn't even know its proper name. Why did Emrys wish to keep all knowledge of it from her? Or her from it?

Well, with luck she would soon know, and in the meantime she enjoyed the journey to that presumed award. The day was sunny and brisk, the trees aflame with oranges and yellows and reds. Truly, this was the most beautiful of seasons, even if it did presage the inevitable cold and death of winter. She was smiling, she realized, smiling as she'd rarely smiled before. It felt good to simply *be*, and to be free. It felt good to be *alive*.

And now, too soon, she almost felt, the village was just ahead.

The very first person she encountered was a young boy, enamored by some dead thing by the side of the road. He glanced up as she passed, stared at the stranger for a moment as children will do, and then dismissed her, returning his attention to the much more fascinating subject of death.

It was her second encounter which threw her.

A woman, carrying a basket of onions. Autumn barely warranted a glance at first, but then the woman did a double-take, and gasped, and very nearly cried out, dropping her basket in her fright, her mouth working silently even as her spilled onions rolled about in semicircles in the dusty road.

Autumn froze, stared at the woman.

"Ach, nein! In the light of day, yet!" the woman croaked, staring in abject horror.

"Do you gape at my eye?" Autumn asked calmly. "The scar that mars my lip? Remnants of a childhood trauma, no fault of my own, and it is quite hurtful of you to stare!" Emrys' suggestion, these words, meant to elicit sympathy and trump rude curiosity. They did not work. If anything, the onion woman was even more aghast.

"It speaks!" she wailed. "A spirit in the full of day, singling me out! Oh I am lost!" She fell to one knee, only barely managing not to collapse entirely, right there in the road.

"Are you mad?" Autumn asked, stepping forward to help the woman then thinking better of it.

"What goes on here?" someone called out; a short, stocky man, barreling towards them. "Leave her be, then! Who are you?" This latter directed at Autumn.

"What's your..." He froze, mid-step. "*Gott in Himmel*," he whispered.

In a tiny village, even the mildest of ruckuses quickly draws attention, and in moments a small crowd had gathered. All of them, to the man, stared at Autumn with a mixture of awe and terror.

"Run to the church and fetch Father Ruttman!" someone ordered a young boy, slapping the boy over the head with his cap for emphasis. The boy tore off like a shot.

"What want you here, amongst good, God-fearing folk, spirit?" someone asked.

"You're mad, all of you!" Autumn said. "I am no more a spirit than you! Look!" She reached down, scraped a palm full of loose dirt from the road, and let it sieve out between her fingers.

"The resemblance is uncanny," someone else said, and the crowd began to relax, a little.

"Who are you?" yet another demanded. "Where are you from?"

"I..." Autumn hesitated, suddenly unsure of herself.

"She looks just like 'er, she does," the onion woman was saying, regaining her composure. "The near spittin' image, aside from her eye, the poor thing."

So that was it, then. They'd recognized in her visage the woman she had been before; the remnant of the lost life upon which her Emrys had constructed her. It was no wonder they'd thought they were seeing a ghost.

And no wonder Emrys had not wanted her to come here. She'd been a fool. An impetuous fool.

The crowd was beginning to disperse, those with better things to do, at least, drifting away.

"You could be her sister," the onion woman said, approaching Autumn without fear now, flustered and apologetic. Autumn knelt and helped her collect her onions.

"Who?" Autumn inquired. She could not help but ask. Curiosity had sunk its hooks in deep.

"Herr Frankenstein's poor wife. He's the doctor that lives in the castle south of the cliff; you must have passed it."

"Wife?" Autumn gasped.

"Yes. Such a tragic thing! She was so young, and *beautiful*. Autumn was her name. Autumn Frankenstein."

8

One of the mob with nothing better to do helped her locate the churchyard. She located the crypt herself. It was a smallish thing, modest and dignified.

Autumn Mary Frankenstein, read the inscription. *Beloved wife of Emrys. Pulchitudo incomparabili.*

The date of death was barely a dozen weeks prior.

And only three days before her own "birth".

Seizing the great slab which blocked the entrance she toppled it aside. She stepped over it, into darkness.

The stone where the coffin should have sat was bare. But there were flower petals scattered about, brown and dry and curled. Flowers had been placed here. And there were marks where something had been moved, scraping the stone.

This place had not been erected for eventualities. It had been used.

Autumn Frankenstein had been interred here.

His wife.

She was his wife. His wife, tragically taken from him and then resurrected through his incomparable genius.

So why hadn't he told her?

What was he hiding???

Her emotions churned, and there came upon her something she had never experienced before, at least not in this, her second life: a wanton urge to *destroy*.

She toppled headstones and pulled smaller markers from the earth entirely, hurling them great distances across the yard or into the nearby wood. One she hurled directly through the glass window of the unoccupied church, and so enjoyed the sound of the glass breaking that she followed it inside, there overturning pews and pulling tapestries and artwork from the walls.

"Why!?!" she screamed at the silent wooden figure hanging on the wall, his broken body and scars reflecting her own. "Why did you allow him to do this thing? Where is your celebrated jealousy???Have you no pride?!?"

Spent, she collapsed to the floor and wept, and when she had no more left she smashed her way out of the church through the barred front door and wended her way back via a circuitous route through wood and field and bramble and brier, so that none from the village might see her traveling in the direction of the castle.

The village.

She hadn't even learned its proper name, she realized bitterly.

It was nearly sunset when she returned. They hadn't even noticed her absence.

Dinner was a quiet, perfunctory affair. Emrys was exhausted, distracted, so that he did not perceive the simmering fury that Autumn was at any wise attempting to conceal. They ate in silence.

Until:

"I must travel to London, to inspect and secure our future lodgings. I will be absent for several days. Will you be all right here, with only Pernicus to tend to you?"

The shock she exhibited was quite real, as she could hardly believe her good fortune. He misinterpreted it, however.

"Worry not," he smiled, though it was a bone-weary smile. "I shan't be gone long. The time will fly, and soon enough we will be away this place and beginning our new life, together."

"Of course." Her smile was even more forced, but he scantly noticed. "Of course. I will be just fine. Darling."

Three days later, his departing coach wasn't even off the property proper before she barged into his study and began sweeping the remaining books off the shelves.

"Mistress!" Pernicus objected, rushing into the room. "If you require assistance with the, er, *concept* of packing, I'd be more than happy to help you help the doctor..."

"Don't patronize me, you wearisome sycophant! Where is it?"

"Where is what?" His eyes narrowed. Even his obsequiousness had its limits. He would not be back-talked by this... thing.

"His safe! His hidey-hole! Wherever it is that he stores his papers and such! Men always have papers! Reams and reams of papers! I do wonder if it is, in fact, how they measure themselves against other men?"

"The doctor would not approve of this. *I* do not approve of this."

"My concern regarding what *you* approve of would not overfill a thimble, dwarf."

He quit the room at this, somewhat to her surprise. She continued her search, ripping paintings from the wall, violently clearing and investigating every space that could conceal something behind.

Nothing.

If not here, then where? His personal chambers? The laboratory? If it were the latter she was defeated, for the men had already come in their carts to take those things away. Still, she couldn't imagine that what she sought would be secreted there, amongst his chemicals and his electrical apparatus. No, if not here, then his bedchamber seemed the next most likely. She hurled aside the leather-bound tome she held in her hand and turned...

To come face-to-face with Pernicus, wielding a torch in one hand, oil dribbling off and pockmarking the carpet. The other hand gripped a pistol.

"So now, I knew it would come to this," he sneered, jabbing at her with the torch. "Do you fear the fire, like your vile antecedents?" he laughed as she recoiled from his feint. "They were affronts to God, but the things he does with you are the foulest of abominations! Better you burn now, that he is not cast down later to burn forever!"

"You're mad!" Autumn gasped.

"Me? Mad? I'm the only one here who is not mad! What is it you're seeking, corpse? Money? His scientific secrets? Speak! Speak or I'll shoot and burn, burn and shoot, until there is nothing left of you, and a better place the world will be for it!"

"I seek confirmation of who I am, who I was. Before."

"Ah. So you have begun to remember after all, despite his efforts. Or perhaps have intuited it? No matter. I'll tell you want you want to know, fiend. You are – were – Autumn Frankenstein, *née* Autumn Moss, betrothed of Doctor Emrys Frankenstein, last of the long, long since disgraced family of Frankenstein. Does this satisfy your womanly inquisitiveness? Will you return to the grave satisfied now I put this bullet into your head?"

"But why? If he loved me so that he was compelled to bring me back from the beyond, defy God and Nature so that we could be together again, why hide my true identity from my? It's senseless!"

The dwarf grinned then. A poisonous thing, that grin, inspired by the hurt he was about to inflict.

"Because, foul maiden, he was the one who killed you."

"No!" Autumn shrieked. *"It isn't possible!"* She lunged for him then, but he deftly darted aside and swiped at her with his torch, touching the sleeve of her dress and igniting it, so that the flames raced up her arm and she was hard-pressed to beat them out, finally smothering them with an antimacassar seized from the back of a nearby chair. Already, though, the damage was done, her right arm blackened and charred, the room rank with the pungent stench of smoke and old, burnt meat.

"So, she does burn," Pernicus cackled. "Like any monster. Any witch."

"He will kill you for this," Autumn said, clutching her smoldering arm.

"Will he? Or will he kill you, and then try again? And again? Forever? After all, you are," he snorted derisively here, "'living' proof that the human body can be perpetually restored, even improved upon. Those legs you wear, for example, are much longer than your previous pair. The soul's the thing; far too ephemeral to be recalled with electricity or mended with the scalpel. But then, it's not as if your charms are...intellectual. Heh."

She stared at him, her eyes dancing with fire.

"Would you like to know...why?" the dwarf asked. "Why he killed you?" When she didn't respond, he plunged on anyway. "He discovered that you were with child; the one feat of creation he *cannot* perform."

"I don't believe you," Autumn said.

"It's true. It is why he is the last of the line."

"Even if this were so, I cannot, will not, accept that I, whomever I was before, would deign to betray my husband in such a manner."

"Oh, you were hardly complicit in the deed," the dwarf leered. "You had help."

"Help?"

The little man's leering grin claimed his entire face.

"Soporifics, of course. Soporifics...and me."

The torch he wielded be hanged she attacked him then, fury supplanting sense, and in response he fired upon her, once, twice. The first shot went wide, the second struck her. She felt it, and it hurt, but it did nothing to impede her and then she had him, hefting him aloft with her still smoking arm, the other slapping the gun out of his hand with such force that his wrist was broken. He screamed, shrill and panicky, kicking and squirming in her grasp even as she hurled him across the room, into the stone wall. Bones audibly snapped and he left a red smear as he slid to the floor. He tried to stand, then merely to crawl, but already she was at his side, lifting him bodily into the air and hurling him, once again, into the wall, with so much force this time that the affected bones did not so much shatter as disintegrate.

"Mercy! Mercy!" he somehow managed, blood bubbling from between his lips.

She had none. Scooping him up, she hauled him out of the room, down the corridor, and onto the balcony without. The view here, at the rear of the castle, was spectacular – grey-blue mountains, white-tipped, streaked with autumnal color. Below, the cliff face – racing down, down, into a chasm black as an endless night that might as well have been bottomless.

"Mercy!" Pernicus tried again. "For the father of your unborn child!"

This was not the right thing to say.

With a great heave she sent him over the balustrade, and his diminishing scream could be heard for so long that she fancied she still heard it, just, as she slipped beneath her sheets hours later and tumbled into a long, dreamless sleep.

When Emrys returned days later, he found the castle unusually quiet. No one appeared to meet him, and he was forced to attend to his own bags before sending the coach away.

Confused, and not a little concerned, he stepped inside and discovered—

Chaos.

Everything that could be ransacked and/or demolished, had been. Smashed, torn, cut, broken, or sliced, there was not a painting, furnishing, bit of kitchenware, or book that had not been subjected to untoward violence.

The villagers. It had to be.

Fear seizing his heart, he raced up stairs and down corridors, searching every room, her name flying from his lips.

"Autumn! **Autumn!**"

"Here."

He'd barely heard her, her response was so subdued.

He flew in the direction of her voice, into his own bedchamber, and found her there, seated demurely on the bed. She'd been burned, he realized, and... shot? But this is not what brought him up short. Rather, he found himself staring at what she had apparently done to herself, rather than the presumed violence that had been done to her. The dress she wore she'd cut short, scandalously short, her long legs exposed in very nearly all their glory, and she'd hacked away her beautiful, flowing hair so that what remained ended well above her shoulders.

He went to her, dropped to one knee, took her hands in his own.

"I feared the worst!" he exclaimed. "I'll see them in chains for this! The provincial simpletons! Each and every last one of them!"

"For what?" Autumn asked sweetly. "Destroying your property?"

"Well, yes, but more for what they have done to you!"

"Me? Am I not merely another piece of property? To be discarded and revitalized, again and again, at your leisure?"

"I..."

"Quiet," she demanded, and he was. She pulled him close, wrapped the both of her long, secondhand legs around his waist, and kissed him, deeply, kindling an immediate excitement in him. She was an outcast from the human race, a freak not of nature, but outside of it; she accepted this now, and as such she knew she would never again taste the fiery sensation men and women called *love*. So she took it, this one last time, drawing Emrys within and reveling in her own glorious power over him as he gasped and mewed and finally cried out. "Why did you not believe me?" she whispered into his ear, even as he clung to her.

"I don't..." he began, betrothed to the lie, even now.

"I found our wedding certificate. I found my *death* certificate. Why did you doubt your own wife – yes, even onto murder – when you should have supported her?"

He petulantly disengaged himself from her and stood, glowering and defensive. Locating his trousers, cast aside in the heat of passion, he stepped into them, his countenance reflecting a level of seriousness laughably at odds with the image of a furious man stepping into his trousers.

"This is not the time to discuss it," he eventually decided upon.

"And when would be the proper time to discuss it? At your murder trial?"

His eyes were like daggers.

"How thankless a creature you are to even propose

such a thing! After I have courted public censure, professional ridicule, and, yes, even eternal damnation to right my wrong and return that which I – yes, mayhap in error – did take from you!"

"'Mayhap'?"

"I grant you that. No more."

She slid off the bed, came to him. Raised her chin so that she was looking directly into his eyes.

"Is Autumn Frankenstein, then, not to be afforded at least some justice?" she asked.

"Autumn Frankenstein, the real and true Autumn Frankenstein, is dead. *You* have no more legal standing than a table lamp, or a dish towel. You are...not even human, by even the most fanciful legal definition. You dare admonish me as if I were merely your fiance, your husband, your widower? You forget that I am, quite literally, your creator. Your master."

"No," Autumn said. "It is I, I who am the master of Frankenstein."

And with that she struck, and ended his life, in a manner most horrific, but mercifully quick.

Hours later she stood upon the balcony from which she had hurled Pernicus, and, later, Emrys' body. Her intention, until this very moment, was that she would join them, having first meticulously set a torch to everything inside the castle that would burn.

But now that the time had come, she could not quite bring herself to step off, into infinity.

So much of what she had absorbed from Emrys' papers and books, and internalized in what passed for her heart, these past few weeks, had contended – nay, insisted – with great passion, that life was precious – a rare and glorious commodity, not to be thoughtlessly relinquished. It seemed a position shared by philosophers and scientists and men of God alike.

Could this possibly apply to a *false* life such as her

own? A life that had been gifted... by a devil?

She didn't know.

But, she mused, perhaps she should find out. Whirling around, she plunged back, into the billowing smoke and grasping flames, down the stairs, and outside, where, from a safe distance, she watched as the heat building within burst the downstairs windows, freeing unshackled flames to lick up the outer walls. The stone edifice itself would not burn, of course, but everything inside would, perhaps cleansing it sufficiently for the next person or persons who chose to dwell therein.

So, for now, at least, she'd chosen life.

And if it was not for her, well, then oblivion was always close by, waiting.

The mob took his head.
He didn't take it laying down.

HEADLESS JACK

(Part 1)

1 - Headless

Your name is Johnathan "Jack" Irving, and you are fleeing for your life. Struggling up one length of winding hillside road, practically flying down the next, the car behind you gaining on you and losing ground accordingly. The man in the pursuing vehicle's passenger seat leans out the window, revolver in hand, but decides not to risk it, instead urging the driver to take ever greater chances. There's no guardrail. As you well know as you make a wild turn, too fast, hugging the hillside, skidding in the loose gravel. A smart mouth and a dismissive attitude don't go well with owing dangerous men money, you reflect, and if you get out of this you promise you'll file that lesson away for future reference. But for now you concentrate on your driving, because if you can

35

just get out of these damn hills, into the city, they don't dare take a shot at you or try to run you off the road. You can lose them in the impenetrable maze of alleys in Chinatown, or even abandon the car entirely and flee on foot. Wend you way back to your room, gather your meager belongings, and skip town, now, tonight. How long is Diamond's reach, anyway? Certainly not to New York, or Miami. Actually, Miami would be kind of nice this time of year. Miami, you decide, it is.

You just have to not die in the next several minutes.

Another turn coming up. You downshift and drift into the left lane to hug the hillside, determined to put more distance between you and them on this next downslope. You make the turn without incident, and...

Some damn fool has stopped their delivery truck at a diagonal, blocking the entire width of the road.

The truck driver, hovering over his raised hood, snaps his head up and stares at you, slack-jawed, as you stomp on the clutch and the brake, jerking the wheel to the left, towards him but away from the yawning space to your right. But there's just not enough time. Wheels locked, tires screaming, you slide into and partially underneath the truck, relocating your engine to the passenger compartment, sheer-crumpling the top-front half of the car in a dull explosion of glass and steel. The impact propels you through the disintegrating windshield, tumbling over and over, the cool dusk air whistling in your ears, and you have just enough time to wonder that you can still see the pulped remains of your headless body in the driver's seat before everything goes black...

"If this is the latest sex thing," Detective Libbowitz frowned, studying the convoluted contraption the body was strapped into, "I don't wanna know about it." Nevertheless, he knelt down for a closer look, examining the leather straps that held the man firmly in place – at neck, waist, wrists, and ankles – in the massive, wooden seat. Roughly shaped from what appeared to be a single block of wood, it was far too crude to refer to as a chair. Libbowitz eyeballed its dimensions and compared these to the width of the sole entrance/exit. It could have been fumbled in here that way, but it would have taken at least two people, and sure as hell they wouldn't have been able to be sneaky about it. "What's this?" he asked Old Ben, the coroner, tapping the mechanism strapped to the side of the thing. There was a rubber bladder hanging from it, and a tube ran from this to a foot petal on the floor. A second length of tubing projecting from the side of the bladder was snaked down the victim's throat. In addition to the tubing, a New Year's Eve noisemaker had been inserted between the dead man's lips. *Happy 1940!* it exclaimed. Not even twelve hours into the new year and that optimistic resolution was wrong already.

"A foot pump," Ben explained. "Alcohol was poured into the bladder, here, and then pumped through this second length, into the victim's throat."

"So he drowned in booze?" Libbowitz frowned. Frankly that didn't sound like a bad idea, but it was only 10 A.M.

"No," Ben corrected him. "The person or persons who did this made a point of running the tube down his esophagus. From the looks of it, he, or they, took their time, just methodically pumping more and more liquor into his stomach." He indicated seven fifths of vodka, neatly lined up against the wall, all empty.

"All that, huh?"

"All that. Half that is enough to kill a man. Unless he's Russian." Ben chuckled at his own joke.

"So he died of blood alcohol poisoning." Libbowitz shook his head. "Murder by booze. At least it's a nice way to go."

"Actually," Ben informed him, "death via blood alcohol poisoning can be quite terrifying and painful."

"There's always a catch, isn't there?" Libbowitz frowned.

2 - Heartless

"Get that beastly thing away from me!" the man shouts.

The beastly thing in question – tongue lolling, tail wagging, obviously friendly – hesitates even as he feels the hold tighten on his leash.

"Oh, he doesn't bite..." the apologetic owner begins.

"They *all* bite," the first man insists. "I know." He's camouflaging his fear with aggression now, staring daggers at the dog owner, daring him to disagree. The owner has seen that sort of look before, and wisely tugs at the leash, quickly leading the animal away.

How appropriate that you witness this little drama from your vantage point, above. You nod to Cynthia and she nods in return, collecting the Victrola and carrying it back downstairs from the roof. You watch for a few moments longer, to be sure your man is letting himself inside, before following her.

"What is wrong with these lights?!" the man is even now grousing, toggling the switch repeatedly. When he gets no results he nevertheless strides confidently into the darkness, through an open doorway he can't see but knows with intimate familiarity is there, only to come up short halfway down the lengthy corridor beyond, shouting out in confusion and surprise. Only these, not pain, yet.

"What in the world? Damn it, why the hell.. what is... Ouch!"

Behind him, you close the door, and lock it. It's your own lock, only just this evening installed, by yourself.

"Gah!" the man in the hallway cries out. "It's

everywhere!"

On the far side of the locked door, you unhurriedly open a single window, allowing just enough ambient moon and city light in so that you both can see. Again, you nod to Cynthia. She smiles demurely – such a lovely smile – and removes the record from its paper wrapper. She moves to place it on the Victrola only for you to silently get her attention, indicate with a twirl of your finger to flip the disk over. The other side. Of course, she smiles. She loads the record, proper side up now, on the spindle, then begins to crank.

"What... what's that?" gasps the man on the other side of the locked door.

Dogs, a half dozen of them or more! Barking, snarling, no doubt slavering! And coming his way!

He whirls, in a blind panic, away from the metallic tangle blocking his path, and tries instead to flee down the cross corridor leading to the kitchen, only to discover more of it there, clogging the space, choking it. But the hounds some madman has unleashed in his house are coming, coming to kill him, and he has no choice, barreling into it, caught almost immediately like a spider in a tangled metallic web. But he can't go back, he can't! Not with those vicious jaws waiting for him! So he fumbles and struggles on, all but swimming through the stuff, more and more enmeshed with every move he makes, hopeless entangled now, the barbs and edges biting into him, slicing his flesh, his hands and face slick with sticky blood. He howls now, oh how he howls, flailing helplessly, impossibly trapped, death by a thousand-million tiny cuts...

You wait patiently until the shrieks reach a crescendo, then indicate with a stroke of your fingers across your throat for Cynthia to stop the record. Nodding, she removes the needle, turns the record over, and cranks it up again. A waltz, this time. It's an original piece, unusually somber, but perfectly danceable.

You set your arms in the traditional position and Cynthia steps into them. Around and around the foyer you twirl to the strains of the untitled piece, accompanied by your victim's screams.

"God in Heaven," Libbowitz breathed. He glared at the two officers already on the scene. "Isn't anybody going to cut him out of there?!"

"We, er, can't sir," one of them explained. "It's barbed wire, sir. Like in the war?"

"But it's a kind I've never seen before," his associate jumped in. "And I grew up on a cattle ranch. Thicker, this stuff. The barbs are a lot sharper too. You'd never want barbs that sharp. It would injure the cattle."

"We're going to need special tools to extract him from that tangle," the first officer concluded. "What's left of him."

Libbowitz was barely listening at this point.

"Why is it painted green, I wonder?" He wasn't asking anyone in particular, but the second officer took up the challenge.

"It's a mystery all right, sir. You wouldn't want green cattle wire because the cattle might not see it. You want them to see it, and learn to avoid it, not stumble into it."

Libbowitz looked closer. The clumpy bits he'd initially taken for pieces of the victim were, in fact, actually welded to the wire. Large red blossoms, cast in iron, the petals razor sharp.

"Rose bushes," he realized. "The damned stuff is designed to look like a mass of rose bushes."

"Cattle might know enough to avoid rose bushes, at that," the second cop mused out loud. "What with the thorns and all."

Libbowitz sighed.

"Who found the body?" he asked the least dumb of

these two men.

"The, heh, housekeeper." Why was he smirking? "We fortified her with a tip from the liquor cabinet and put her in one of the bedrooms to calm down."

Libbowitz suspected they'd fortified themselves as well, which explained a lot.

"Take me," he said.

The "housekeeper" looked like she wasn't even old enough to be drinking alcohol, and her uniform left very little to the imagination. No wonder she was so distraught; she'd clearly lost more than an employer.

"In your own words," Libbowitz repeated soothingly.

"I arrived at the usual time... Could I get another n-, er, drink?" she asked.

"Get her a glass of water," he ordered one of the uniforms. This clearly wasn't what she'd meant, but she didn't press the issue.

"Anyway, I arrived at the usual time, and the first thing I notice was that the door was ajar, and that made me really nervous because Mr. Spence, well, he's an important man, right? He's got enemies."

Libbowitz extracted a pad and pencil from inside his overcoat and doodled, pretending to take notes.

"So I peek inside," the girl continued, "and in the foyer" – she pronounced it like it rhymed with *lawyer* – "I see the Victrola, set up on its own little table, right there in the center of the room. Now I thought that was a little strange, you know? I mean, maybe he had some friends over, but why would they bring their own Victrola and why would they set it up in the middle of the foyer? Nobody would be able to hear it from there."

"So it wasn't Mr. Spence's Victrola?"

"It wasn't." She considered. "Unless he only just bought it late yesterday, I suppose." She wiped a tear from her eye with the handkerchief she was holding. "He was always buying nice things on a lark. That's why I liked him so. Liked working for him, I mean."

"Where's this Victrola now?" Libbowitz asked no one in particular.

"Oh, we moved it into the kitchen," one of the uniforms informed him. "To get it out of the way."

"Of course," Libbowitz sighed.

The Victrola itself wasn't much to look at, and it certainly didn't tell him anything, but the record on the Victrola was almost certainly a wealth of information, if only he could parse out what it might mean. The label on the side facing up was decorated with the image of a single red rose. There was no title or performer listed. When he wound the player up and dropped the needle into the groove, he found himself listening to a waltz so slow and melancholy that it was almost a dirge. The other side was even more perplexing: an image of a snarling mastiff hound on the label, with matching contents on the record: just snarling, growling dogs, the volume steadily increasing, as if they were getting closer. The quality on both sides was quite good – very near lifelike.

He lifted the needle from the record.

Truly baffling. What could it all mean?

3 - Hapless

"Got some more out of the maid," Beant said, straddling the chair across from him.

Libbowitz looked at him questioningly.

"That thing uptown. Guy tangled up in wire in his own house?"

"I wasn't aware you were on the case," Libbowitz frowned. Beant, pronounced *bent*, was a solid detective, but he was still young enough to be eager, and he thought he was funny. It was an annoying combination.

"The chief, he'd thought maybe we'd work together on this one."

Libbowitz sighed.

"So, I took the maid out for drinks," Beant plunged ahead. "Nice girl. Wants to be a nurse. I think that's pretty swell. Anyway, she told me that Tam Spence, our dead guy, had an irrational fear of dogs. What they call a phobia, I guess; nightmares and everything. Seems just the sound of a pack of dogs was enough to send him into paroxysms of terror."

"So our killer, or killers, played the record to drive him into the wire." Libbowitz leaned his chair back on two creaking legs, considering this. "Spence had some serious criminal ties so I'm not entirely surprised at the viciousness of it, but it still seems like an unnecessarily complicated way to kill someone."

"Right. Which means whoever did it must've hated him like the Good Lord hates a sinner."

"Well that's something, at least. We haven't had any luck identifying the manufacturer of the wire, and the record player is a standard model, available anywhere."

"What about the record itself?" Beant asked. "Can't imagine that's a popular title: 'Slaughter, and the Dogs'."

"We haven't had any luck with it either. There's no publisher listed anywhere on the thing. No manufacturer. No catalog number. Nothing."

"Maybe it's a one-off," Beant suggested. "A custom job."

"Can't be too many places that do that," Libbowitz nodded. "You attack that angle. I'm gonna check in with some of my less reputable contacts, see if they can tell me whose feathers Mr. Spence might have ruffled."

"Voice-O-Graph," the fellow said, like it was a bad word.

"I should know what that is?" Beant asked. The two men stood in the lobby – if you could call it that – of a shabby little recording studio, nestled between two warehouses on the East Side.

"An abomination is what it is," the engineer snorted. He was a small man, prematurely balding, nervous and irritable. "It's going to kill the industry, mark my words. Why buy a record when you can record your own?"

"How does it work?" Beant asked. He'd never heard of the thing.

"You step inside a little booth, like a picture booth, warble your fool, off-key heart out, and it impresses your questionable contribution to the arts onto a six-inch disk, suitable to gift your Great Aunt Sally or, better yet, use as a drink coaster."

"And anyone can do this?" Beant asked, scribbling the name of the device down.

"Anyone with no shame."

"The recording we're trying to identify featured a full orchestra and, er, animals. I doubt they were all crammed into a space the size of a photo booth."

"Do you have the record with you?" the engineer asked.

"Right here." Beant extracted it from the leather briefcase at his feet and handed it over.

"No sleeve? You really ought to store it in a sleeve."

"Sorry."

The man held it up and examined it carefully. "Ah, yes, see right here?" he said. He pointed to a series of numbers scratched into the surface of the disk, in the space between the label and where the grooves ended. "These are matrix numbers, and can they tell you all sorts of things. The catalog number. The take."

"Where it was recorded?" Beant asked hopefully.

"In this case, yes. Well, sort of. If you're in the know."

"Could you be a little more vague?" Beant prodded.

The engineer smiled. He seemed quite pleased that his expertise was proving useful in an actual police investigation, and he wanted to milk the experience for all it was worth. "This string, right here," he explained. "The number series 00013000. That's a sort of coded signature, see? If you're in the know. 'Lucky' Dan Dodds. He recorded your platter, so he can almost certainly tell you who's performing on it."

"This Lucky Dan, you've never met such a character," Beant laughed. "He's worked with so many crazy musicians – famous ones, too – I'm surprised he can keep the stories straight."

"But he remembered the record?" Libbowitz asked.

"He did indeed. Said he wouldn't forget that session if they took his brain out. A half orchestra crammed into his studio...a pack of rambunctious dogs, complete with handler...highly specific instructions regarding the musical portion of it...it's an original composition, he told me...meat brought in for the dogs... Like a three-ring circus, he said."

"But who *ordered* the record produced? Who was it *for?*"

"Oh, yes, sorry. It was a girl. Red hair, intense, very pretty. Paid in cash. Signed the bill with an X."

"I hope you got more of a description beyond 'very pretty'," Libbowitz frowned.

"I did indeed, right here." Beant passed his notes over. "'Very pretty', that's the important bit though. I'll be on the lookout for that."

"I'll bet you will." Libbowitz glanced over his scribbled observations before tossing the notebook back to him. "While you were casting about for your next drink date, I was doing some policework. Remember that fellow last month, the one who died of a forced alcohol overdose while strapped to a chair?"

"Of course. That one's come to a dead end, I understand."

"Well, seems he and our wire victim had something in common. They were both known enforcers for the Diamond gang."

"And you think..."

"I do. The crimes are equally diabolical and convoluted, and equally vicious. Might just be a flare up of inter-gang warfare, but it seems much too personal for that. I think our killer or killers targeted these individuals specifically, over a specific grudge, a specific incident. My only question is this: Have we reached the end of it, or is the whole Diamond gang on the menu?"

4 - Heedless

"Mr. Diamond! Mr. Diamond! A moment, if you please!"

Nils Diamond froze in his tracks, glowering. Whoever it was, they'd managed to catch him in the scant few moments after he'd left the sanctity of temple but before he reached the safety of his car.

"It's the Sabbath," he reminded the man puffing to catch up with him. "I don't discuss business on the Sabbath."

"This isn't exactly business, sir," the man informed him, flashing his credentials. "Finley Libbowitz. Police detective Finley Libbowitz. I'd like to ask you some questions..."

"I'll bet you would," Nils Diamond cut him off. "Talk to my lawyers."

"Wait, just a minute sir, please." The cop was gasping for breath, his hands on his knees. He was embarrassingly out of shape. Nils Diamond was a stoutish man himself, certainly no Johnny Weissmuller, but even he found this detective's physical condition embarrassing.

"Seeing as I can clearly extricate myself from this conversation by leaving at a brisk walk, I'll give you one minute. But I hope you plan to do all the talking because I have nothing to say."

"Thank you, sir," the cop said, straightening his tie and pulling himself back together. The icy wind whipping in off the lake seized his hat just then, and he had to chase it down.

"Forty seconds," Nils informed him when he returned. Libbowitz didn't beat around the bush.

"Mitchell Dunas and Tam Spence," he said.

Nils Diamond stared at him blankly.

"Do you know them?" Libbowitz prodded.

"Should I?" asked Diamond. "I told you; you talk, I listen."

"Well, sir, I think you do. Or rather, did. They're both dead, you see, under very unusual circumstances."

"That's unfortunate," Diamond said.

"One of them," Libbowitz persisted, "was tied down and forcibly poisoned. The other was done in with barbed wire, inside his own home."

If this information affected Diamond in any way, he didn't show it.

"We're well aware that they've both done...work...for you in the past. We've a theory that someone might be targeting your, er, organization."

"I'm fully capable of handling my own affairs," Diamond replied.

"You could be next on their list," Libbowitz pointed out.

"Fully capable," Diamond repeated. "Your time is up. Good day, Detective."

Three weeks later Nils Diamond arrived at his legitimate place of business to find the office in a mild, bemused uproar.

"But where did it come from?" someone asked for the umpteenth time.

It was a huge, rabbit-shaped something, wrapped in shiny foil, the foil printed with a full-color image of a grinning, anthropomorphized rabbit, wearing a jaunty yellow-plaid vest and holding a pocket watch. Broad as a good-sized man, it was at least seven feet tall, if you included the ears. Miles Parks, the first person in that morning, had found in standing in the middle of the lobby, despite the fact that the front doors were still locked and, so far as he knew, no one besides himself and Mr. Diamond had a key.

"The tag on it says 'To: N. Diamond and Assoc. For: Services Rendered'," one of the secretaries repeated for Mr. Diamond's benefit.

"A client, obviously." Miles frowned, baffled. "Strange that they didn't take any credit for it."

"Maybe there was an explanatory note that got lost, or is being delivered under separate cover," someone suggested.

"It smells like, well, chocolate."

Nils didn't like this. First of all, literally everyone was gathered around the thing, rather than working. Second, the whole situation gave him a funny feeling, a sort of instinctive twinge, one he'd felt more than a few times in his life and had learned to listen to. After all, any of his regular clients knew full well that he didn't celebrate Easter. That meant that this was either a weird joke, some sort of obtuse message, or something stranger/worse.

His employees were all looking to him now. Obviously they'd been waiting for him to arrive and make some sort of decision.

"Well, Mr. Parks, open it up," he said, forcing a grin. It all seemed harmless enough, on the surface. Still, he took a step back as Miles used his pocketknife to carefully peel back some of the foil.

"Sure, enough, it's chocolate!" he exclaimed. "Happy Easter, I guess!"

"Easter is two weeks away," Alice from accounts pointed out. She was the recognized office killjoy.

"Well they certainly couldn't deliver it on Easter proper," someone else noted. "We'll be closed."

"What, uh, what shall we do with it, Mr. Diamond?" one of the secretaries asked.

"Well, I certainly can't eat it all!" Nils laughed.

"Unless maybe it's one of those dishonest hollow ones!"

"Nope," Miles confirmed, gently rocking it back and forth. "Solid as a rock! Or a block of chocolate, anyway!"

"Well have at it, then!" Nils told them. "A treat for the entire staff! But please, can we all get back to work?""

"Thank you, sir!" several people grinned simultaneously. Miles used his knife to cut slivers and wedges of chocolate for anyone who wanted some, then broke off one of the bunny's sizable ears, wrapped it in paper, and stashed it in his desk. "For my kids," he explained.

Everyone settled back into their usual Monday morning routine, and the office was quiet for the next hour or so. Until just past nine o'clock, in fact, when Nils heard a woman scream, immediately followed by the sound of something sizable toppling over and taking several smaller somethings with it. He grabbed the pistol he kept in the top left drawer of his desk and burst out of his little office at the rear of the building, ready for anything.

No, not quite anything.

Not Alice, in a dead faint on the floor, the unconscious sweep of her arm having taken half the contents of Jerry's desk with her as she fell. There was a wet smear of chocolate across the front of her yellow dress, and more chocolate was running down the side of the huge bunny and pooling up at its feet. Apparently it had a liquid center, and when Alice had prodded too deep with Miles' knife...

"Jesus in his Heaven," Richard Ames whispered, "that's not chocolate." He took an instinctive step back. No one was helping Alice off the floor.

Slowly, carefully, Nils approached the chocolate rabbit, his pistol at the ready, as if afraid the massive candy bunny might suddenly pop to life and turn on him.

Blood. The chocolate rabbit was full of...blood.

Someone – Nils didn't look up to see who – gagged, ran for the toilet, and almost made it.

"Call the damn cops," Nils said, smarting at the sound of his own voice. He'd never uttered those words, never, not once in his life, and he never thought he would. "Somebody call the cops."

5 - Humorless

"It's high quality chocolate," Beant said, examining the bunny from all sides.

"I concur," one of Nils Diamond's employees interjected. Undeterred, he was still munching on a piece he'd broken off prior to Alice's grisly discovery.

"Are we done with this guy?" Libbowitz asked the uniformed officers.

"We got his statement, yeah," one of them confirmed.

"Then get him out of here!" Libbowitz stalked over and snatched the chocolate out of the man's hand. "And stop eating my evidence!"

One of the uniforms escorted the man out. Besides the police, Nils Diamond was the only one who remained in the room.

"Okay, Detective, you were right," Diamond fumed. "I'm ready to accept police protection."

"Very generous of you," Libbowitz said, making a show of looking the chocolate bunny in the eyes. "Any guess who we're gonna find inside this thing?"

"How the hell should I know?"

"Maybe check the bottom of your shoes," Beant suggested. "Has anything you stepped in this morning gone missing?"

"My shoes are as clean as my business," Diamond snorted. "And my conscience," he added, before one of the detectives could say anything.

"What if the chocolate's poisoned?" Beant mused instead.

"Hadn't thought of that," Libbowitz considered. "I wouldn't think so. I think it's meant to send a clear, straightforward message, and that's the whole of it. Still, it might do for anyone who ate some to get their stomach pumped."

"Your staff's gonna love that," Beant grinned at Diamond. "Hope your lawyers' pencils are all sharpened."

"This is a fucking nightmare," Diamond groused.

"Murder usually is," Libbowitz agreed. "Maybe you want to point us in the right direction before there's too many more?"

"Get in here!" Chief Dickson barked the second Libbowitz walked in the door. "You too, Beant!"

He stepped into Dickson's office, Beant trailing behind.

"The Dispatch is calling 'em the 'Holiday Murders'," Dickson said, slapping the morning edition onto his desk. *Creamy Confectionery Contains Corpse* the headline blared.

"They do love their alliteration," Beant said.

"I'm glad you're finding the humor in it, Beant. You kept that roses-and-wire job out of the papers, you couldn't do the same with this one?"

"There were a lot of witnesses this time, Chief," Libbowitz explained, "and Beant couldn't wine and dine all of them."

"Some of them were men, sir, and I'm not that way," Beant added.

"This is just superb. Glorious. Do you two clowns have any leads at all?"

"Well sir, the guy baked into the big bunny was Talbot Evans, a low-level thug in the sometimes employ of Nils Diamond, which pretty much confirms the primary theory we'd been pursuing. As such, we're working closely with Mr. Diamond to see if we can determine who else might be on this lunatic's list and hopefully head off the next one."

"You're 'working closely' with a known gangster." Dickson sighed heavily. "This just gets better and better. Incidentally, Ben tells me that your latest victim wasn't 'baked in'. Mild burns over damn near his entire body indicate that he was coated with the stuff while it was still pretty warm, and the ultimate cause of death was suffocation."

"They had to have used a mold then," Beant snapped his fingers. "And something like that ought to be pretty unique and not too very difficult to track down."

"I'll need men," Libbowitz told the chief.

"You've got 'em," Dickson said. "This is sick stuff, and the press is ecstatic. The mayor ate half my face off this morning. Maybe try and make some progress before I suffer a stroke, eh?"

6 - Harmless

Cynthia meticulously lines the figurines, each approximately one foot tall, on the mantle for your approval. You nod. Yes, yes, these will do nicely. You especially appreciate the attention to detail. Each little character is unique; you can almost identify which one would be the leader...the studious bore...the wag. They would probably be quite successful as characters in a newspaper comic strip.

These particular characters have a much more important task to perform, however.

"Mitchell Dunas," Libbowitz began, "our alcohol victim, was discovered on the first of the year and had only been dead for a few hours. Tam Spence, the man who suffered death via a thousand tiny cuts, courtesy a barbed wire rose bush, met his maker late on the evening of February thirteenth, so, essentially, Valentine's Day. So far, so consistent. Our killer is employing a holiday motif, and killing his victims on or very near that holiday. But this last one breaks the pattern, if it even was a pattern; Talbot Evans was suffocated in chocolate no earlier than March eighth, probably over the weekend of March nine-ten, to be delivered to Diamond's office on Monday the eleventh. Easter isn't until the twenty-fourth."

His four-man team listened intently. Also attending the meeting were Detective Beant, and Nils Diamond.

"Maybe he knows we're onto him," one of the detectives, Lorenzen by name, suggested.

"Except we're not onto him," Beant said. "We *think* he's targeting Mr. Diamond here, and/or people associated with Mr. Diamond, but that's purely conjecture at this point."

There was some eye-rolling and smirking amongst the four. They all knew who Nils Diamond was.

"Okay," Libbowitz said, "keep it to yourselves. The law's the law and murder is still illegal, whether you have issue with the victims or not."

"And as to this *him* business," Beant added. "So far our sole person of interest isn't a he, it's a she. Red hair, worn short in the current fashion. A looker. That's all we've got."

"I'll tackle that angle," another man, Morey, immediately volunteered. The group laughed.

"Everyone's to tackle that angle," Libbowitz told them, "because it's all we've got. That and finding out who manufactured our giant Easter Bunny mold. Now get to it."

With that, the meeting was adjourned.

"You know," Libbowitz suggested to Diamond as the men filed out, "if you were to provide us with a signed confession listing every crime you're directly or indirectly responsible for, it might help us compile a proper suspects list."

"Yeah, you'd like that, wouldn't you?" Diamond said. "Too bad for your investigation that I'm as clean as a newborn baby's bottom."

"At least answer this," Beant requested. "Do you happen to know any homicidal redheads?"

"Plenty," Diamond laughed. "But none with beef against me. Both my ex-wives are blondes."

Security detail on Nils Diamonds' estate wasn't such a bad gig, usually, but ever since a parade of guys Diamond had previously engaged the services of started getting blipped, Jackie had been assigned to walk the actual grounds, outside, and it was cold and damp outside this time of year, and he hated it. It so infuriated him towards those dead guys that if they weren't already dead, he'd take 'em out himself.

He sighed, buttoning up his coat and then, less than a minute later, unbuttoning it again. The air bit with winter teeth, but the sun beat down from a clear sky, and the two were clearly at war, with him stuck in the middle.

Goat shit is what it was. Complete and utter goat shit.

His third time walking the perimeter a splash of color caught his eye at the other end of the flower gardens, closer to the house, and from sheer boredom he decided to investigate. Some sort of pedestal, that he was (maybe) certain hadn't been there on his last pass, had sprouted up right in the middle of one of the frost-covered hollyhock beds. Marching straight across the rear lawn, he came up on the thing and, sure enough, there sat a three-foot faux-Grecian column pedestal, slathered in red paint, where he was absolutely sure, now, one hadn't been before.

Atop it stood a ceramic statue, about a foot tall, of a leprechaun. The red-bearded, green-clad little mick, thumbs hooked in his big black belt, hat askew, wore a grin like he'd just eaten the cat. A short legend appeared on the molded scroll unfurling at his feet: *ME GOLD IS NOT BEHIND THE GARDENING*

SHED!

Jackie pondered what he was looking at for a good five minutes.

Nils Diamond was not a funny guy. In fact, he was maybe the least funny guy Jackie had ever worked for. He didn't like funny gimcracks, and he didn't play pranks, and he wouldn't employ anyone who did horse around or play pranks.

So what in fuck hell *was* this?

Maybe, *maybe*, if he'd been instructed to look out for "anything unusual", he might have played it differently. But he hadn't, and Jackie Lemon wasn't all that great at convergent thinking, or critical thinking, or any kind of thinking, really. It wasn't what he'd been hired for.

The only part of this his brain was effectively processing was *behind the garden shed*.

Something was behind the garden shed, that maybe oughtn't be.

He decided to investigate. After all, he had a gun. And anyway, what harm could a goofy little statue portend?

Wending his way along the garden paths, in no particular hurry, he made his way to the shed.

Nothing out of place. He tried the shed door first, in case someone was hiding inside, but it was locked, and when he peeped through one of the dust-caked windows, shielding his eyes from the incessant sun, there was no one there.

Only now did he look behind the shed, and while he wasn't particularly concerned, yet, he did keep his hand on his piece.

There was another pedestal, this one painted orange, with another leprechaun perched on top of it. This one was different from the first, however: it wore a mildly irritated expression, and held a single finger in the air as if *tsk-tsking* him. Also there was something underneath it, peeping out from beneath its base.

A coin.

Cautiously, Jackie tilted the figure back and retrieved the coin.

Was it...? He bit into the soft metal with his teeth.

Holy shit. It was real. Real, solid, 24 karat gold!

He turned the coin over, hoping to identify it, but both sides were blank.

A scroll featured at the bottom of this statue too. This one read: *ME GOLD IS NOT FOR YOU! YOU'LL FIND NO MORE NEXT TO THE FOUNTAIN!*

Jackie immediately made for the garden fountain, not dawdling this time.

Another pedestal, yellow. Another leprechaun, its countenance more irritated than the last. Another coin. Another message: *KEEP YE AWAY FROM THE ORNAMENTAL GATE!*

Jackie excitedly followed each clue to the next, from the yellow pedestal to a green one, then blue, then indigo, each one rewarding him with another gold coin, each one leading him further and further from the house.

The penultimate message directed him into the copse of elm trees situated at the extreme end of the property.

Now, he hesitated.

He drew his piece.

He reflected, to the best of his limited ability.

He even considered going back to the house, for some backup.

But that penultimate message had referred to the fanciful leprechauns' *hoard.*

A *hoard.*

Slowly, carefully, he eased his way in, amongst the trees.

There was a bit of a clearing, sort of, at the center.

And in this clearing, a final, violet pedestal, with one last leprechaun, this one seated, arms crossed, its face a mask of rage. There was no hoard – no coin, this time, even – but there was a rolled, vellum scroll, tied with a purple ribbon, weighed down by the little statue.

So that was it. A message for Mr. Diamond, no doubt. All this rigmarole had been to lure him away, maybe, or just to prove some sort of point. He had no concerns about the former – there were plenty of other men patrolling the house and grounds – and points, well, even the most pointed of them were harmless enough, in and of themselves.

Jackie smiled at his little play on words, and strode forward to retrieve the message.

And fell, with gut-dropping suddenness, right through the ground, into the narrow, covered pit he hadn't been savvy enough to be looking for.

Narrow it was, too: he could barely even move his arms, even though he'd instinctively thrown them into the air as he fell and now they were above his head. And it was deep: nine feet, about, leaving only his panicky, waving hands above ground level. He was trapped, but good. And he'd dropped his piece.

"Help!" he hollered, knowing it was probably no use. "Help!!"

God but the ground was cold. And hard. It couldn't have been easy to even dig this damn hole.

"HELP!!!" he tried again, because why not?

Something blocked a portion of the branch-dappled light dribbling in from above, and with some difficulty he craned his head to see who or what it was.

It was a girl. Pretty but harsh, with electric blue eyes and shortish red hair so dark that it tended towards black. She frowned at him as one vaguely disappointed with a foolish child.

"Lady!" he called to her. "You gotta help me!"

She tilted her head at this, like a curious puppy. Then, after a moment she disappeared.

"Yeah, go get a rope or something!" he encouraged her.

Nothing for a couple of minutes, then he heard

something bumping along the ground above, like a heavy, wheeled object being pushed or pulled into place. It came to a stop near the hole, but out of his line of sight. Several clangs, some clicks, the sound of tinkering. What the hell was she doing up there? "Lady!!" he shouted. Her face reappeared, briefly (she looked annoyed), then disappeared again.

Now he could smell something. The unmistakable smell of, well, heat. Something metal being heated up.

Jackie Lemon began to get scared.

"Lady!!!" he shouted, futilely struggling and thrashing in his frozen-earth prison. "You better not do nothing stupid! I work for Nils Diamond, see, and he's not someone you wanna mess around with!!!"

The redhead's face appeared a third time, accompanied by another.

Jackie gasped.

This guy – because it was a guy – looked like something out of a dime novel. He wore a black suit, accented with a black tie, black gloves, and even a black cape, but that isn't what had taken the gangster's breath away. No, what had taken his breath away was the huge jack-o'-lantern mask the guy was wearing – a huge jack-o'-lantern mask that Jackie could swear **was on fire**.

"It ain't possible!" he gasped. A standard-issue mook wearing a mask that was on fire, his fucking head would burn up! That meant this wasn't no person; it was a ghost, or the Devil himself come to personally drag Jackie to Hell!

Jackie lost his mind at this point, screaming and crying and struggling impotently in his earthen prison.

Coolly, methodically, the pumpkin-headed "man" positioned something at the edge of the narrow pit. Intense heat was absolutely radiating off...whatever it was...and Jackie was quickly drenched in sweat. Gloved hands grasping a long, iron handle, the pumpkin man tilted the thing – it was a sort of cauldron, Jackie could now see – and poured its luminous orange-red contents into the hole.

It was gold. Molten gold.

Jackie Lemon didn't even have time to scream.

7 - Hopeless

"His body was mostly reduced to ashes," Beant explained, "but the gold that was dumped over him solidified quickly enough that Ben was able to pour sculptor's plaster into the mold it created and get a passable impression of the guy's face; good enough for his wife to identify him, at least. Johnathan 'Jackie' Lemon. Now she's fighting with the city because she wants to inter the gold cast of his head because 'it's all that's left to bury' but the city doesn't want to give it up."

"Mr. Diamond couldn't confirm that it was his man without going through all that?" Dickson asked.

"A bunch of his boys have cut and run," Beant explained. "Could've been any one of a dozen guys."

"They've definitely deviated from their pattern," Libbowitz frowned. "The killers."

"Did they? Saint Patrick's is just a few days off. And what makes you suddenly so sure it's *they*?"

"That big, iron, smelting contraption. Two people to move that thing, at least. So, *they*. And Saint Paddy's is before Easter, but they did Easter first. Which means they're not inflexible, not obsessively locked into any specific order or pattern. I was hoping that might be how we'd get 'em. Now, I don't know."

"We've got Slotnick and Drayton tracking down the crucible," Beant said.

"We already know what they'll find," Dickson fumed, irritably drumming his fingers on his desk. He looked like he wanted to strangle somebody. And was his face always that red? Beant couldn't remember. "Ordered and collected by a beautiful redhead, who paid in advance, in cash, and didn't give her name. To hell with the equipment; where they got the gold, that's what I'd like to know!"

"Well there isn't any significant amount missing, so far as we can determine," Beant said. "We're working that angle too, of course. Sir."

"That girl, she's the key," said Libbowitz. "She is the key. If we could just identify that damned girl...." He drove his right fist into his opposing palm.

"Diamond's howling for protective custody," Beant decided to mention. Libbowitz cringed. Now was *not* the time to be shoveling it on, not with the mood Dickson was in.

"God, isn't *that* ironic?" Dickson snarled. "Set him up in the cheapest, dirtiest, dingiest hotel you can find. One with bedbugs, if possible. Assign Drayton to him and tell Drayton I said so if he bristles."

The lights, powered by electricity stolen from the building above, flicker, briefly painting the subterranean chamber in staccato shadow. Somewhere, the incessant *drip-drip-drip* of a leaky water main–or perhaps just condensation–continues. Enough to drive one mad, that dripping. Twenty years ago this was to have been a high-end lounge for an underground railway that never happened, and you've furnished and decorated it accordingly, although the dark and the damp have already taken their toll, reducing the fine pieces you acquired and installed here, at great expense and inconvenience, to so much rubbish. And displaying the Van Eyck panel demonstrated an inexcusable lack of judgment; already, the dank environment has caused it minor but irreparable damage.

Truthfully, you resent these accommodations; they're far too *Gaston Leroux* for you.

Nevertheless, they offer ample space, the necessary seclusion, easy access to power, and have thus far proven impossible for the authorities to locate. These things, of course, are considerably more important at this juncture than comfort, or even aesthetics. One must be prepared to make compromises if one is to achieve anything of consequence in this life. Only a fool believes otherwise.

Speaking of which.

My April Fool, you think. *I'd like to inspect my April Fool.*

Across the room, Cynthia, lovely Cynthia, nods, as if she can hear your thoughts. Retrieving the prototype from a darkened alcove she reverently carries it across the room and presents it to you. A classic jester's motley: yellow with orange spots in the style of a giraffe's; floppy hat, a bell culminating each of its three points; jutti shoes, also belled; garish gloves; a full face mask.

Perhaps...a little more gaudy, yet, you communicate to her, and she smiles in agreement.

Sometimes it's invigorating to let loose, go a little wild, and sweep good taste aside.

"I had an idea," Beant said, dramatically dropping a massive box of files onto Libbowitz's desk.

"A good one?" Libbowitz asked, one eyebrow raised.

"I think so, yeah. We've scoured the files for redheads, right? You even had Morey digging through the traffic stuff, just in case. It's clear our mysterious beauty doesn't have a criminal record, at least nothing we can find. But I got to thinking..."

"Uh oh."

"I got to thinking: all these crazy, convoluted murders, they took some serious planning. Between designing and acquiring the customized equipment and learning the daily habits of the victims so as to strike with maximum efficiency, we're talking a considerable amount of time invested, even for a team of people. That, I realized last night, was the key: time. I don't think our redhead has enough hours in the day to participate in this complex, ongoing scheme *and* meet her own personal obligations, whatever those might be. Husband, boyfriend, family, friends, employer... *someone* has noted her absence. And maybe they've reported it."

"Missing persons!" Libbowitz smiled. "Watson, you are brilliant!"

Brilliant it might have been, but it was tedious work. It was over fifteen hours later, technically morning again, when Beant disgustedly tossed the latest report he'd been examining back into its box.

"By the way," he said, "I'm pretty sure I'm Holmes and you're Watson."

"That been bothering you all day?" Libbowitz asked, groping for a grin but immediately giving up on the idea. He'd done his share of desk duty, but right now the bones in his *fingers* hurt, and that was definitely a first. Maybe he was developing arthritis. The idea didn't depress him near as much as it probably should.

"This would be a hell of a lot easier if we knew who we were looking for," Beant sighed. "My kingdom for a name."

"Every case would be a lot easier if we knew who we were looking for," Libbowitz reminded him.

"When we're done I'm gonna reorganize these files by hair color," Beant promised. "For next time."

"If there's a next time, I'll put in for early retirement. This is hopeless. Let's call it a night."

"You sure?" Beant sounded disappointed.

"I'm not finished with the idea, I'm just dead on my feet. Or my ass, as the case may be. How many more of these damn boxes are there?"

"Seventeen, twenty."

"Christ. Tomorrow, put Slotnick on it. He's been getting too much fresh air."

"He's not gonna like it."

"Yeah? Well tell him shit doesn't roll uphill."

8 - Helpless

Two days later Drayton sighed heavily as he played his four-thousandth game of solitaire. He should've brought a book, he reflected. He wasn't so much about books, really, but almost anything would be better than this endless, stifling quiet. Nils Diamond didn't talk, didn't complain (much), didn't want to play cards. He just lay there, stretched out on the bed, hands behind his head, thinking. About what, Drayton couldn't imagine. Also for the four-thousandth time, he wondered what he'd done to piss off his superiors so that they saddled him with this lousy babysitting detail.

There was a light rap on the door.

"That must be our food," Drayton said to Diamond, to no response. He swiped the cards aside to make room, rose, drew his Colt just to be safe, opened the door without undoing the chain, and peeped through.

He nearly took a step back, he was so startled.

"What?" Diamond asked, noting this. Drayton grinned.

"You're not gonna believe this," he said, undoing the chain and flinging the door open.

There, balancing a covered tray of food on one hand, was a...child?...midget?...dressed just like a court jester from ye olden days, belled hat and shoes and all! A white mask concealed his face. Smiling, Drayton relieved him of the tray, turned, and set it on the table. Diamond was actually sitting up now, on the edge of the bed, intrigued by this touch of weirdness.

"This a novelty place?" he asked, referring to the hotel. "You put me up in a novelty place?"

"Wasn't my call," Drayton told him. The jester was still standing there, waiting. Did you tip midgets? Drayton wasn't sure. More importantly, if he did tip would the department compensate him for it, or would they tell him that it was an expense he took on of his own volition?

Something really weird about this midget, too, Drayton reflected. The way he stood, moved. It was...off...somehow, and it gave him the willies.

Holy shit.

Slowly, lest he startle the jester, Drayton reached down and tugged at the rubber mask, which came off easily in his hand. He breathed a sigh of relief; the kind of relief you feel when the explanation for something unnervingly bizarre turns out to be mundane and perfectly logical.

The "midget" was a monkey. Drayton didn't know what kind of monkey, exactly–that was the kind of information one found in books–but it was definitely the kind they trained to ride unicycles and smoke cigars and do all sorts of other tricks. So these folks had trained this one to deliver lunch. Clever. Weird, but clever.

He handed the mask back and the monkey took it.

"Well, thanks, monkey," Drayton said. He presumed this meant he didn't have to tip. "Sorry there's nothing for you, but I don't have change for a banana." He could've sworn the monkey looked disappointed, but regardless at this admission it turned and ambled off towards the stairs, in that bow-legged way that monkeys do.

"I hope he didn't touch the food," Diamond said. He lifted the cloche to take a look. "Unsanitary."

"Weird is what it is," Drayton said. He reflected on that for a moment. Libbowitz had repeatedly drilled it into him that he should report anything weird that happened–anything at all–immediately. Did this count? A monkey delivering sandwiches? It was weird, sure, but leaning more towards ridiculous than concerning. He didn't want Libbowitz yelling at him again. Libbowitz had been yelling a lot, lately. "Maybe I oughta call it in," he mused out loud, half hoping

Diamond might offer an opinion on the matter.

"Maybe you should," Diamond agreed, unhappily chewing his roast beef on rye. "Tell 'em we need a patrol car out here immediately. Tell 'em to bring some decent sandwiches. These taste like a bad hoax gone awry."

No, Drayton decided, he'd better not call.

Still...

He knew what he'd do. He'd go down to the lobby and ask the hotel clerk about the monkey.

"I'll be right back," he told Diamond. He'd drawn his Colt without even realizing it.

Slowly, he re-opened the door and stepped out into the hallway. It was empty. The monkey was long gone, and, so far as he knew, they were the only people on the second floor. He eased down the hallway, descended the stairs, Colt at the ready, feeling more and more foolish by the second.

No one in the lobby, either. Not even the clerk.

"Fine time to take a break," Drayton grumbled.

Motion to his right and behind. He spun around.

Another monkey, this one also dressed as a fool. He knew it was a monkey by the way it stood and walked, and he knew it was a *different* monkey because it was considerably taller than the first. He approached it, reached out with his left hand, and pulled away the white mask, its features frozen in their eerie, permanent grin, and found himself looking into an equally unnatural grin radiating from a goofy orange face.

An ourang-outang. The smaller one that had delivered lunch, then, must have been a chimpanzee.

The ourang-outang curiously reached for his gun and he gently guided its hand away. He counted himself lucky that the monkey didn't insist. They were powerful creatures, he recalled, and could easily kill a man...

Could easily kill a man...

Dressed as a fool...

An April fool, perhaps?

He turned and bolted for the wall phone.

"Hillvale police station!" he nearly shouted into the receiver.

"I have no listing for that number," the operator informed him in pleasant, clipped tones.

"Are you daft? Of course you do! HV6-1971!"

"I'm sorry, sir, could you check your number again?"

"Is it your first day!? Gah!" He hung up. He'd grab Diamond and get him out of here, call from a phone on the street. Whirling around, he tore past the indifferent ourang-outang and back up the stairs, skidding to a halt when he found himself face-to-face with yet *another* masked and costumed jester-monkey, this one larger even than the last, hunched over in the way of the great apes, arms danging, head canted curiously. It didn't advance on him, but it was blocking his way. "Diamond!" he shouted down the hall. "We're leaving!"

No response.

Carefully, he edged his way around the big ape. Was this one a gorilla? No, it was much too skinny to be a gorilla. Still, the idea of a gorilla lumbering around unchecked was more than a little unnerving. For the monkey's part, it paid almost no attention to Drayton at all. Good, the man thought. Let's keep it that way.

Drayton's thoughts turned to the room, now, and what he might find inside. God, if Diamond was dead in there he might as well resign, because Libbowitz would never let him hear the end of it...

Behind him, unseen, the hunched-over "gorilla" slowly straightened up.

April fool.

Did he hear something? Behind him?

Drayton spun around as something flashed in the jester's hand. Too late, Drayton realized that this one was no monkey, but a man. But he barely had time to chastise himself before the blade flashed forward once, twice, and expertly opened the policeman's throat from ear to ear.

To be continued...

SPECIAL SCIENCE BUYS! AMAZING OFFERS!

Cryogenics. DIY step-by-step guide $5. Head only, $2
Time travel is real! Don't worry, you've already written us for more information
Resonator. EZ instructions, build at home. Activates at the flick of a switch. Go ahead, turn it on. Nothing bad will happen.
Radioactive material. Grab bag. $10
Beautiful women want to meet you! Box 129 for more information. Not vampires or killer robots from the future, probably
Learn to speak Sumerian! Free pronunciation guide
Triffid seeds. Easy to grow. Delicious. Friendly
Earn florm in your spare time. No limit. Serious inquiries only.
Can you decipher the code? Fun new puzzle game! Write c/o FBI Headquarters, Wash. DC. Not a job offer.
Scholastic Stamina Test (SST). Strategy guide/tips. Top scores guaranteed!
UFOs are fact! That's it. That's all I've got

The Great Dragon Burlesque Show of 1953

I could've sworn I heard him right when he initially invited me.

"Not really my thing," I told the enlisted man. This was Korea, tail end of the war. I was a civilian, but my duties intersected with the military's, and while I'm not at liberty to divulge exactly what it was I did, I will say that it occasionally inconvenienced the officers and therefore delighted the enlisted men. As a result I was quite popular with the latter, and I counted several friends among them. This one, a reluctant draftee who hated the Army and everything about it, went by the handle "Icepack" and we were, I'd say, pretty close friends. I never knew his real name though.

"It don't mean you're funny or nothing," Icepack went on, anticipating my initial objection. "It's just for fun, you know? Lotta guys are going. A whole group of us." Then he hit me with the clincher. "Beer's cheap."

So that's how it started.

There ended up being six of us, after two bowed out and one got his pass revoked: me, Icepack, "Saint" Clement Boudinot (who was anything but, but professed aspirations to ultimately join the priesthood), Davy "Douchebomb" Hanson, Nick "No Nickname" Mifflin, and I guy who's handle I barely processed then and couldn't hope to retrieve now, but for the sake of clarity I'll call him Klondike, which, if you must know, was the name of a dog I used to own. All five of these guys were privates, regular army, mid-tour and keen to make it out the other side. No delusions or tough-guy posturing here. Just four average Joes, literally. I've sometimes wondered how differently things might've played out if my companions had been, say, recently-minted Marines instead. Maybe a lot better; but maybe way worse, too. Guess I'll never know.

We started the night late in the afternoon, at a place called Stars & Bar, which, as you can probably guess, had opportunistically sprung up to cater to American soldiers. The service was strictly Korean though, limited almost exclusively to shots of *soju* (a grain-derived alcohol that was basically moonshine), and rarely-the-same-twice cocktails concocted from soju and whatever fruit juice or soda pop they had on hand. Their signature drink, which the enlisted boys had dubbed "The Liquefier", consisted of six shots of soju and enough juice and soda to make it taste good. They served this in a tall glass carafe, and wouldn't sell more than two to the same person during the same visit, although if you stepped outside long enough to smoke a cigarette then came back in and ordered a third they pretended like they didn't notice.

By dusk we were deep in the devil-soju's grip, and decided to start drinking our way in the general direction of our ultimate destination, which according to Douchebomb's information was an establishment deep in the black heart of Geumdong. This *dong* – neighborhood – was technically off-limits to military personnel, as it was dense with hookers often barely out of their single digits, and the worst kinds of drugs. The ban was only barely enforced, though, and we didn't anticipate any problems.

It's to laugh, now.

Third watering hole after the Stars & Bar, the trouble started. Well, not really started. What happened there was more of a harbinger, you might say. (Yeah, I looked that word up; and you can, too.) It was a two-story place, the bar proper upstairs, the owner and his family living downstairs. You had to tramp right through their living room to get to the stairs, but they didn't dare swap it out because there was this wonderful open balcony at the rear of the building that gave you a pretty spectacular view of... well, mostly alleys, to be honest, but in a place like that not many buildings had big, open balconies, so it was a definitely a novelty, and people would buy more drinks when they could quaff them outside, sitting on that wonderful balcony. We were doing that very thing when Icepack spotted her.

"Look at that little slice of F.E.H." he said, leaning *way* over the cheap metal railing. It creaked ominously, but ultimately decided to support his weight. This time. F.E.H., incidentally, was Icepack's term for any local gal who happened to catch his short-lived fancy. It stood for "Far-East Heaven". He campaigned like crazy to get it to catch on, but no one else ever adopted the term so far as I know.

"She is a tasty one," Clem agreed, adjusting his glasses. He needed bifocals but steadfastly refused, preferring to slide his current pair up and down his sizable nose, as needed.

The girl was beautiful, no doubt about it. Twentyish, hair black as night, skin a creamy mocha that defied any immediate presumption of race. She might even be a white girl, I thought, even as she sensed our shameless stares, looked right up at us, and frowned. Blue eyes. Well, that settled that. She wasn't dressed like a Korean or an American, but rather kind of European. But not classy *ooh-la-la* European. More the kind of European girl you only saw in the right sort of movies, if you get what I mean. Everything short and high-slit and tight and low-cut. I'd say her outfit didn't leave much to the imagination, but truth be told I was imagining quite a bit just then, and I'm sure the other guys were too. Even as I processed and filed all of this she stopped, flipped us off with both hands, then cut down the alley running alongside the opposite building, consciously adding a little extra swivel to her hips. The boys applauded and cheered. Hell, I cheered, and I'm usually above such things. A beat-up old van had been backing down the alley, which was way too narrow for it, and now it blocked our view. *"Boooooooooooooooo!"* Klondike hollered through cupped hands. Nick thoughtlessly lobbed his half-empty beer glass in the van's general direction.

The van slammed on its brakes.

We heard the glass pop-explode on the pavement as four small Korean men spilled from the cab of the van.

"Oh, shit," Nick breathed. There was no question we could take them. The question was how much trouble everyone would get into after.

But it turned out they didn't give two wits about us, although one of them, who'd seen where the flying beer had come from, shot a narrow glare in our direction.

They were after the girl.

Instantly three of the men had her in their grasp, kicking and screaming, while the fourth jerked the rear door of the van open.

I never saw men move so fast.

Not the kidnappers. My boys.

Instantly, Douche and Nick had hurtled the railing onto the low roof of the building next door, and were leaping from there to the ground. Clem, a considerably less athletic fellow, clambered over the railing as best he could and hung-dropped into the alley. Me and Klondike, not quite prepared to do either of those things, turned and dashed down the stairs, through the ground floor, and out the front door.

All of us were a bit too late.

Already the van was tearing off, one of the men in the back struggling to pull the door closed from the inside even as their thrashing victim landed a kick square in his face. Douchebomb was in hot pursuit on foot, just shy of an arm's length away, Nick right behind him. Clem was rolling around on the ground, clutching his ankle. The van picked up speed, fishtailing slightly in the process, losing its rearview mirror with a *crack-pop!* as it collided with the left wall, plowing through some indifferently stacked crates and sending the cat that had been hiding inside one of them yowling off in search of safer cover. Klondike and I made a halfhearted effort but there was no way we were catching up now that it was reaching speed, and even Douche gave up as it hurtled out of the alley, bottoming out in the process, trailing sparks and scattering pedestrians as it cut a hard right and tore off down the street.

"Fuck!!!" Douche shouted, looking around for something to throw at the fleeing vehicle and failing even at that.

Witnesses, and more who wished they had been, were already appearing out of the woodwork. Two of them were helping Clem to his feet. The rest chattered excitedly amongst themselves or asked us, in Korean and broken English, what, exactly, had happened.

"They grabbed that girl!" Nick kept telling anyone who would listen. "They grabbed that girl!" Probably most of them didn't understand him, but they frowned and nodded sagely anyway.

We spent the next two hours explaining what had happened to local law enforcement, and let me tell you, that'll sober you up quick. The evening had inarguably taken a sour turn.

"White slavers," Clem muttered for the hundredth time since we'd disentangled ourselves from the authorities. It was well after sundown, and we were still drifting in the general direction of the show we'd set out to see, repeatedly delayed by the countless drinking establishments that kept getting in our way. We were drinking in earnest now, but not getting drunk, scrabbling for the light mood the kidnapping incident had thoroughly dissipated. "Mother fuck!" Clem brought his fist down on the table hard enough to make our glasses jump, also for the hundredth time.

"Fuck, but she was beautiful," Icepack lamented, toasting the air in her honor with the lukewarm beer in his hand and then finishing it off in one go.

"I'm never gonna forget her eyes," Klondike said. "Never seen that color of blue before. God *damn*, those eyes were somethin' else..."

"Don't use the Lord's name in vain," Clem grumbled.

"Don't take it personal," Nick said irritably. "He doesn't know yer gonna be Pope someday."

"Hey, Clem," Douche grinned, locking hands behind his head and leaning his chair back on two legs. "Do you know what kind of pussy you can get in a convent?"

Clem glared at him through narrowed eyes.

"Nun," Douche finished.

This was the turning point, I realized. Everyone

was angry and wound up, frustrated and deep in that dark kind of drunk that simmers ineffectively all night long then hits you all at once like a runaway tank. If Clem starting swinging, it was all over, and we'd probably wrap up the night in the custody of the MPs.

I wasn't the only one who realized this, I think, because everyone got deathly silent, the sort of silent that muted everything else around us so that it felt like we were the only five men in the world. Everything beyond our table, for all practical purposes, ceased to exist, a murmur-blur at the edge of our sole focus: Clem. Would he escalate the situation? To what degree? And for God's sake what was he waiting for?

Clem stared at Douche for what felt like an eternity.

Then he grinned.

Then he laughed out loud.

Only then, when I started to relax, did I realize how much I'd tensed up. My muscles hurt.

"Asshole," Clem said.

And that was it. The gloom was dissipated.

"One more round!" Nick exclaimed, slapping his palm on the table. "And then were gonna go see us some cross-dressing comedy!"

We barged through the narrow, crowded streets now, on a mission. The city took on an unfamiliar, repetitive quality. Every street seemed the same, every corner a duplicate of the last, leading to still more corners that would be duplicates of the current corner. No one spoke English. Shrugs when Douche mangled the half-remembered name of the supposed venue where this show was purportedly being held, blank stares when we asked where the drag and burlesque was. But fate was on our side, or maybe against us, because despite all odds we found it, a sizable building impossible – and yet somehow equally easy – to miss, crouched deep in shadow as if hiding, ready to pounce. Yong-ui. That was the name of the place. Douche had been asking after *Hong-ui*, which is probably why no one had known what we were talking about. They charged us obscenely at the door but we were excited to pay, lambs skipping our way to the slaughter and happily coughing up for the privilege.

Maybe if we weren't so drunk we'd have picked up more on just how not welcome we really were, but we were and so we didn't. The interior was set up like a supper club, with a low, wide stage up front. The kind of stage you'd perform a full-scale play on, the Korean version of Macbeth or something. They'd constructed a stylized but intricate set on this stage, a sort-of medieval village setting, inexplicably skewing European in its particulars but with distinct Korean touches as well. An idealized culture meld. I suspected that this meant much of the comedy would be at the expense of westerners, which made sense. Maybe that's why they were a little put out by our presence, I concluded at the time. Possibly they were afraid we'd take umbrage, and start trouble.

After a brief argument amongst the staff two of them took responsibility for us and steered us towards a big round table somewhere midway between the stage and the back. It was large enough to seat more people, but even as the place filled to capacity and beyond no one joined us. Lots of folks were standing. Cheap cigarette smoke collected beneath the ceiling and hung over the room like an acrid haze.

We ordered a round of soju, shots. The girl who served us had a smile that seemed plastered on. But she wore her hanbok short, showing off an impressive length of leg, so we barely noticed.

Two rounds later the lights dimmed, and a short blast of American rock 'n' roll clawing its way out of a row of dilapidated speakers hanging from the ceiling announced the beginning of the show. "More skin!" Nick demanded through cupped hands, before anyone had even appeared on stage.

Now two actors trod out, and while I'd wished more than once over the course of this weird night that we'd invited a translator along with us, never more than over the next several minutes, as we slowly came to realize that this show wasn't just a a parade of slapstick and farce, which translates pretty smoothly across all cultures, but had an actual, in-depth *plot*. Oh there were definitely broad comedic elements – one character dropped things and fell on his ass a lot – but on the large it seemed more like a riff on the whole epic "knights of old" thing, with an appropriate European flavor but all mixed up with Korean tradition too. Maybe? Honestly, I don't think the boys much cared. They laughed when the comedic relief fell down, hooted and whistled and double-slapped the table whenever a pretty girl made an appearance, and with that they seemed pretty much satisfied. But me, for some reason I wanted to know what was going on, what it was all *about*.

In hindsight, even moreso.

To keep it simple, it seems there were these two guys. One of them was clearly your stereotypical Sir Lancelot type, a bit pompous but obviously meant to be a stand-up guy. His buddy/assistant/sidekick was a klutzy buffoon, full of withering observations judging by the timing of crowd's laughter. They wandered from town to town (represented by slightly altered variations of the same stage-settings, quickly rearranged during brief curtain drops), trying to do good deeds but always messing it up, somehow. Most times they ended up chased out of town by the locals, hauling ass in circles around the stage in a slapstick manner that got old pretty quick. I studied the crowd during one of these repetitive scenes, tying to fathom their apparent attitude towards this whole, underwhelming spectacle. They laughed during the presumably funny parts, sure, and ogled the pretty girls, a bit, but mostly they seemed to be... waiting. For some big, amazing climax, maybe? Could it be that all this nonsense was building up to something considerably more entertaining than the sum of its parts? I sure hoped so.

"Bring out the drag queens already!" Douche suddenly bellowed, echoing another thought I'd had. For a drag and burlesque show, this really didn't feature a whole lot of either. Maybe the sidekick's incomprehensible-to-us witticisms and overall jackassery fulfilled the comedic requirements, and one pretty young thing did lose her top at one point, reacting with exaggerated surprise and dismay even as my boys lost their minds, but there hadn't been a queen to be seen. Unless some of the tiny little Korean girls up there, in their even tinier little outfits, were men in drag, and I can assure you with a fair amount of certainty that they were not.

Maybe we'd bumbled our way into the wrong venue. Or maybe Icepack had just plain misunderstood.

I checked my watch. We'd been here for almost two hours, and even given my dim understanding of what was going on onstage I could tell that the story, such as it was, was careening towards some sort of conclusion. Maybe the brave knight would take on a whole gaggle of drag queens for the big wrap-up. That made about as much sense as anything.

God, but we were drunk. Even I was drunk, really drunk, and I usually don't find myself that far gone without realizing how I got there. Rounds just kept coming, courtesy the girl in the too-short hanbok. I lost track of who was paying.

The mayor – I presumed – of the latest medieval village our heroes had wandered into was making all sorts of grandiose promises, it seemed, and punctuated this by casually pouring an entire bag of gold coins into the knight's outstretched hands. The sidekick directed a witticism directly at the audience, punctuated with an exaggerated wink, and then scrambled for the coins which had fallen to the ground.

The knight accepted this final job, thrust his prop sword dramatically into the air, and once again the curtain fell.

"You better be hiring him to impale a bunch of drag queens!" Douche shouted. Man really wanted to see his drag queens. And watch some of them get impaled, apparently.

The curtain was down for a considerable amount of time, this round. If you listened, you could hear the hands back there, hurriedly redressing the stage. It sounded like they were really doing it up for the final scene; a whole new set, maybe, as opposed to another slightly re-imagined town. The room had grown strangely quiet, aside from our rambunctious party. Everyone else seemed to be waiting with bated breath. It was as if the entire show up to now had been politely tolerated; a necessary, reluctantly suffered prelude to this moment, the big finale, the epic showstopper. In the immediate hindsight of that inexplicably crystal-clear moment everything that had come before felt... *ceremonial*, somehow, even obligatory. Like when your parents remind you that you have to go to services before you can open your Christmas presents.

I felt suddenly uncomfortable. Not because we were there, because no one seemed to mind *that* much that we were, but because we were the only ones hooting and hollering and carrying on and making a drunken spectacle of ourselves.

The girl in the short hanbok had vanished. They weren't serving us anymore.

A tinny, scratchy fanfare belched out of the speakers, was clumsily cut off, and the curtain finally began to rise, slowly.

Even our party shut the fuck up then.

The new set – a cavern, piled high with papier-mâché and cardboard treasure – was a degree nicer than the ones that had come before, but hardly anyone noticed, I suspect.

All eyes were understandably drawn to the **gigantic lizard** on stage. Real. Breathing. Alive.

"It's a fucking *dinosaur*," Clem whispered. Once he was able to pick his jaw up off the table, of course.

He wasn't wrong. I mean, that's what it had to be, right? Because there just aren't any non-dinosaur lizards that get to be twenty-plus feet long, even if they do drink their damned Ovaltine.

It didn't look quite like any dinosaur I'd ever seen a picture of, though.

It certainly had the overall *flavor* of a dinosaur, one of the low, squat ones that presumably ran about on all fours. But it had a sort of frill down its back, and its face was too long, somehow, more like a wolf than a reptile. And it had these... things on its head. Long, thin, ending in a sort of curlicue, they weren't ears or horns or anything else I could immediately identify. Whiskers, maybe? Antenna? I couldn't wrap my head around it then and I never did figure that bit out. As for the other important particulars: it was sort of green-brown in color, with streaks of red down its scaled body, and was currently bound via a massive chain to a huge staple set in the floor of the stage. I'd vaguely noticed the staple before, because it was a permanent part of the stage and had been incorporated one way or another into all of the sets. Realizing that this was almost certainly its primary purpose was a bit of a mind-blower.

Someone at our table – I didn't catch who – gasped as the impossible beast slowly tilted its head first one way, then the other. I don't think any of us could quite process that it was really real, and not some sort of incongruously professional prop or illusion.

"Holy shit," Icepack breathed.

That's when I realized how still the room had gotten. Sure, we'd been the loudest jokers in the place up to now, but there had always been that underlying rustle-murmur you get whenever more than a few people are gathered together in one place. No one was talking now. No glasses clinked. No one scooted their chair or shifted their weight. I found myself looking around, away from the wonder on stage, taking in the room, because that silence just didn't scan right. Probably in that moment I was acting the better soldier than the actual soldiers I was sitting with. The people around us, Koreans to the man, weren't paying us any attention, though, nor were they as surprised as we were. No, they were leaning forward and staring in what was clearly *anticipation*. This was it, I realized. The reason they'd all come here tonight, paid their cover. Just to see this thing sit there, on stage? I wondered at this. There had to be more to it.

Unfortunately, there was.

After a longish pause in the onstage action, no doubt intentionally included for effect, the show went on.

Some of the villagers from the village our heroes had just visited, along with their mayor who was so loose with his gold, marched onto the stage, a prisoner in tow. This was not only a new character, but a new actress, one we hadn't seen before.

Except, me and the boys, we had seen her before.

Even now, decades later, I'd recognize those astounding blue eyes anywhere.

"What the dripping dick?" Douche gasped.

Blue Eyes was still wearing the outfit she'd had on when she'd been snatched off the street, but it was sliced and torn now, not randomly but with meticulous care, a stagy attempt to make her look bedraggled. Her struggles seemed real enough, though, and she let out a particularly keen wail when she laid eyes on the big lizard. For the lizard's part, it perked up considerably when the girl entered the picture. Up to now it'd been perfectly docile, but her presence very much energized it and now it climbed to its feet, sniffing the air and shaking its head back and forth as if trying to cast off the remnants of sleep or some narcotic.

There was a wooden stake set into the floor, and the girl was roughly lashed to it.

Someone in the back of the room shouted a few Korean words of encouragement.

Clem was on his feet, I realized, and I seized his arm.

"It's just a show!" I hissed, even though I wasn't all that sure myself, now.

The lizard lumbered its way across the stage. The chain was just long enough to allow it to reach the girl. The other actors scattered and disappeared into the wings.

Blue Eyes screamed, and I knew, absolutely and without a whisper of a doubt. Because no one is that good an actor.

Icepack, Douche, and Klondike were rushing the stage even as Blue Eyes began coherently shrieking for help in what, to me, sounded like French.

Two big guys – big for Koreans, anyway – appeared out of nowhere and tackled Douche to the ground. The crowd went wild, some jeering, others egging the other two Americans on. Icepack catapulted himself onto the low stage, Klondike right behind him, even as the great reptile opened its maw, revealing row after row of vicious teeth. Too many rows of those, this thing had. Like a shark.

Both men froze then, clearly having no idea what to do next.

I was on my feet, too, finally, and so was Nick. Men were rushing us from all sides, trying to keep us from the stage. Clem slugged one guy, and Nick easily dodged a punch so clumsy and ill-considered that the guy throwing it ended up face-down, on the floor.

Up front, the actor playing the knight had appeared, and was struggling with Klondike, trying to push him back off the stage. Klondike pummeled the guy, relieved him of his wooden prop sword, and then rushed the lizard.

With a weary snarl, the lizard opened its mouth wide and...

Okay, I know you're not going to believe me. I can accept that. But its true, so help me God and all the Catholic Saints and, hell, all the Korean gods too and any other gods you care to throw into the mix. It happened.

That big, honking reptile *belched fire all over poor Klondike.*

He screamed, horribly, because fire is a bitch of a way to go, and then he dropped to his knees, still hanging on to that smoldering wooden sword, the front half of him charred black from head to toe. And I guess that salamander preferred its meat cooked because it forgot all about the girl for the moment, advanced on Klondike, plunged its foremost teeth of its lower jaw into his stomach, jerked its head in a practiced motion that deftly sliced the man wide open, and immediately went to town on the steaming, half-roasted guts that spilled out.

Douche immediately puked all over the guy he was struggling with.

The rest of us stared in shock, awe, dismay, about a dozen other emotions from that subset.

A not insignificant portion of the crowd was cheering.

The girl keep yowling and babbling in (probably) French, and I think she spit up a little, too.

One of the Koreans was waving a gun around now, a little thing, and Nick managed to grab it.

"No-Nick!" Clem shouted. "Right here!" Clem was halfway to the stage now, bowling men over, and he was the acknowledged best shot among them.

The pistol tumbled through the smokey air, too

high, but Clem's freakishly long arm was up to the challenge. He snatched it out of the air, stiff-armed another Korean aside, aimed the gun at the lizard, and fired.

At that, people started bolting for the exits. A pissed-off, carnivorous dragon is one thing, maybe too esoteric to properly be afraid of. But everybody knows get get the hell out of the way when bullets start flying.

Clem's first shot missed by a country mile, but his second and third struck true, hitting the scaly beast twice in the face. It let out a furious roar that sounded more like an angry toot – it reminded me of a foghorn – before angrily swiping Icepack off the stage with one of its front claws. He landed hard, on his back, knocking the wind out of him. Clem had the good sense to duck then, and it probably saved his life because that monstrosity let out another belch that blasted the table behind him, exploding a bottle of liquor and setting everything around it aflame. As it was, he still lost most of his hair.

Whereas the audience fleeing in a semi-orderly fashion before, now pandemonium ensued.

Koreans were racing in all directions, even towards the stage, trying to get away from the rapidly spreading fire. As always happens, men went down and were trampled when they needn't have been, if everyone had just kept their wits about them. Not that I felt any pity for these men, who had presumably paid good money to watch a fellow human being get eaten alive by a monster.

Icepack, even as he gasped for breath, was clambering back onto the stage.

Nick had been swept up in the fleeing crowd, dragged in the direction of a side exit. Clem was beating at his smoking hair. I had no idea *what* had happened to Douche. "Ice!" I yelled. "We gotta get out of here!"

No dice. He was going for the girl. And I'll be

damned if he didn't make it, diving over the big lizard's snapping tail, darting across the stage, and immediately attacking her bonds.

Jesus Christ. The *walls* were on fire.

Never, and I mean never, exhibit a fire-breathing dragon in a venue constructed entirely of alcohol-soaked wood. That really ought to be Dragon Wrangling 101.

My lungs were burning, my eyes were burning, even my ears were burning from the litany of vile and surreal swears and blasphemies coming out of Clem's mouth the likes of which I've never heard since, and I've worked oil fields, side-by-side with longshoremen, and I ultimately married a middle school teacher. I don't know if Clem ever did become a priest, but if he did that string of expletives alone must've set his ordainment back a decade.

And then, somehow, I was outside.

The building was an inferno, and something inside, something not human, was screaming. Not hissing or roaring or howling. Screaming. Like a person. It was unbearable. I couldn't get away from that sound fast enough, but really I never did get away from it, not entirely. It resurfaces every now and then, when I'm stressed or overworked, in my absolute worst dreams. Already dozens of people were on the scene, desperately dousing the neighboring structures with buckets of water in an unsuccessful attempt to keep the conflagration from spreading. In the end, half the street went up. Eventually I found Nick and Clem found us and then we all found Douche. The four of us double-timed it out of that place without once looking back.

The Army ultimately concluded that Icepack and Klondike were dead, having burned up inside one of the many bars that had previously lined the decimated street, because that's what the other three men told them. They took the hit for being in a dong where they oughtn't't've, said admission lending just enough credence to the rest of their story. So far as I know, no one involved ever told anyone else what really went down that night. Not being bound by military prohibitions myself, I made an attempt to visit the burned-out wreckage of Yong-ui, a couple of days after. Not sure what I was hoping to find. Icepack? The monster's skeleton, openly smoldering in broad daylight? I dunno. It didn't matter anyway because the whole block had been cordoned off and the bored BNS officers babysitting the barricade wouldn't let me anywhere near the place. Less than a week later I picked up an assignment on the other side of the planet, practically, and the head office wanted me there yesterday. I never even had a chance to swing by and say "So long!", and I never saw any of those guys again.

So that's it. That's what happened. Sorry if the ending wasn't pulp-hero enough for you, or that I didn't tie up all the loose ends in a neat little bow. Sometimes life doesn't supply you with all the answers, and something this weird, I think it's important to tell it just how it was, without embellishment, so that someone smarter than me can maybe dig in and really figure it all out someday. Bit of a postscript, though. I said I never saw any of the guys from that night again and that's true, but maybe five years later I was working a job in Mali when a letter with about a million different postmarks on it found its way to me via an old acquaintance, who'd been holding onto it for me for some time. Inside was a brief note, wishing me well. It was signed, simply, "Ice". The note was accompanied by a photograph, crumpled and water-damaged and already faded. It was Icepack, all right, posing with, I presume, his wife and their two young children.

All three of them had the most striking blue eyes.

I, Werebear

SNARE of the WEREBEAR

1

How long until I give in, I wonder? Already my hands are shaking. And, God help me, it's right there, on the decking beside me. How I wish I'd stashed that hooch somewhere a little less accessible, or at least less visible. Maybe inside one of these empty, sea-damp crates I'm lurking behind. I'm not about to try to stash it now though, because once I'm holding that smooth, silver flask in my hand there's no way I'll be able resist twisting it open and...

And I can't, not yet. I have to wait, just a little bit longer. So I can make him pay.

2

Probably I should start at the beginning.

I'm a hunky, and while I'm not particularly proud of it I ain't ashamed of it neither. My Pa, he tumbled right off the boat and into a factory that worked him eighteen, twenty hours a day, six a week, until he kicked over stone dead, an old, *old* man at forty. He looked more like eighty. Four years ago, that was, and ever since me and Ma and my little sister Agnes have been on our own. I was fifteen years old at the time, and I decided right then and there that the factories weren't going to happen to me.

So I made do. Didn't have no use for school but that was no big thing because not so many of us did. Hunkies, I mean. Weren't but two, three kids I knew who'd even seen the inside of a school. Hell, most of 'em worked the factories, plenty of them the very one that claimed my Pa, and they were, to the man, fifteen or sixteen or twenty on the inside but thirty or more to look at from the outside, usually within a year of walking through those big factory doors. Like I said, not for me.

And that *not for me* approach might've served me just fine, for the foreseeable future, seeing as I lived with my Ma, and she didn't charge me but nothing to live there, and loved me too much and missed my Pa too much to ever toss me out, even if maybe she ought to've.

Except for one thing.

I love, and I mean love, the drink. That initial, hot snap as it hits your tongue and slithers down your gullet; the warm feeling that all but permeates you as it starts t' work its magic; the almost supernatural change in your outlook when it finally takes hold. Glorious. Spiritual, really. I do believe, in a sense, it's a religion, or enough akin to one that maybe that's why proper religious folks, them that's forever "Jesus this!" and "Jesus that!" and "Jesus t'other!" are always throwing such a hissy-dilly over it. After all, nobody likes competition. Fortunately, my family never was much for any of that Jesus stuff. "Life is hard!" my Ma always says. That's her religion. Not me. A couple, three toots and life stops being hard real fast, and suddenly, no matter how bad you was feeling five minutes ago, life's a party. That's *my* religion.

As you can imagine, the most powerful challenge

to my faith was God-blessed Prohibition. I mean really, who do those Jesus-beaters think they are to deny an honest, hard-working man the harmless luxury of a refreshing drink or two at the end of a long, hard day? Not that I'm a working man, as I mentioned, but I believe, with all my heart, hallelujah, that the very same holds true for those of us looking to put down six or ten over the course of a long, hard night, and maybe a couple more for that doll down the other end of the bar, the one with the skirt that leaves nothing whatsoever to the 'magination and the gams up to her neck. Honestly, there oughta be a law.

Okay, there is a law. You know what I mean.

It isn't that drink isn't out there. Hell, it's practically everywhere, and unless you were making a scene, or colored, or the brass coppers happened to be on the rampage that week, no one gave a rat's biscuit. It's just that you had to put some effort into locating it, sometimes, and it wasn't always accessible the very instant you might need it. And, of course, if you want the Real McCoy – as opposed to some questionable rotgut near as likely cooked up in the same bathtub dear ole granny takes her weekly in – it'll cost you.

That's where I got myself into some trouble.

Boozers can't always be choosers, and I ain't no snob, and no mooch neither if I can help it, but I got a taste for the good stuff, and one day I found myself with the overpowering need to get bent and no way to finance it. Maybe if it had just been me things might've played out different, but young men have a way of goading each other into increasingly questionable behavior, and there were three of us at the time: me, and Kender, and creepy old Petey Prawn.

"You're not looking so well there, Dicky," Kender told me as we walked the river bank, absently tossing stones into the languid water. It wasn't so much a river, really, as it was an elongated pond, in no real hurry to get anywhere.

"Need a drink, that's all," I told him. As a matter of it I had it pretty bad, just then, but I don't think they appreciated just how debilitating my need was, in particular. When you're nineteen years old, you always think you *need* a drink.

"Sick Dick," Pete laughed. That was my nickname, on account of the fact that my family name was Illes. Dicky Illes, that's me. There used to be a little mark above the E in Illes, so that it didn't look and sound quite so much like *ills*, but my Pa had excised that, to "Americanize" it.

"We *all* need a drink," Pete said, proving my previous point. "Trouble is we ain't got but, what, nothing between us?"

"World's fulla money," Kender said. "We just need to figger out how to get some of it."

"Well, there's work," I grinned, and they laughed. This was a common joke between us.

"I'm open t' any *realistic* suggestions," Pete responded.

"Old Spizzer, he owes me some," Kender said, with no real conviction. He was staring out across the water, apparently lost in thought.

"He's no good for it," I reminded him. "And you know it."

"Ought t' bust his head, that one," Pete fumed. "Catch 'im round behind the speak, bean 'im a good one and take that money he owes you."

"I think you might be onto something there, Prawno," Kender said.

"What, take out old Spizzer? For the few measly he owes you?" I asked. I was mildly appalled. He was one of us, Spizzer was, even if he always shirked on his debts. Anyway I was sweet on his older sister, and it probably wouldn't serve me too well in that regard if I dry-gulched her baby brother in an alley.

"Not Spizzer then," Pete shrugged. "Some rando."

"You mean rob someone, actually rob someone, in broad daylight?" I asked.

"We can wait 'til it gets dark," Pete grinned.

"I think you're onto something there," Kender nodded, returning his grin.

"I can't do it, I don't think," I confessed.

"Dicky's terrified. Should've known," Kender said.

"It's too risky," I pointed out. "What if we get caught? Or we, I dunno, accidentally kill the guy?"

"Who said we was gonna target a guy?" Pete leered. I told you he was creepy. And in this case I'm glad he was, because that settled it for me.

"I won't do it," I said.

"Fine," Kender said, mildly disappointed. Aside from the potential windfall, the idea had the flavor, at least, of an adventure, and he was bored.

"What if," Pete ventured after several seconds of silence, "there weren't no chance of someone getting hurt?"

"Like if we had a gun?" Kender asked. He said things like that, sometimes, that only made sense if you understood his convoluted way of thinking.

"No, I mean we let ourselves inside someone's place – maybe old Spizzer himself – and just pick up whatever they happen to have lying around."

"We'd be doing them a favor," Kender agreed. "Straightening up the place."

"Right! Right!" Pete was getting very enthusiastic about this idea.

"Except we'd be on the short list of the first persons they'd suspect," I pointed out.

"I ain't never stolen a thing in my life!" Pete lied, making a show of being highly offended.

I hadn't, at that point, and that's the truth. But the drink was calling to me bad. If I didn't nibble one soon I was gonna be in a bad way.

"It's gotta be outside the neighborhood," I said. "Someone we don't know, and who don't know us."

"And it's gotta be someone what deserves it," Pete

added. "Like a dinge, or a twist."

Like I said, creepy.

"I got an idea," Kender said in that low, cool tone of voice that suggested that he really did have a plum idea, a real sockdolager.

"We're growing older by the minute," Pete prodded him.

"The Hun," Kender said.

The Hun.

The Hun was a bit of a local character, to say the least, who lived on the far side of the old rail yard, in a disused storage shed that no one had the motivation to run him out of. He spent his days collecting scrap tin and old steel cans, glowering at passersby, and occasionally getting into heated, one-sided arguments with the local birds. The story – certainly wrong in almost all of its particulars – was that he was a kraut deserter from the Great War who'd somehow washed up on our shores with a box of stolen German gold, and was waiting it out until he could safety return home with his treasure and live a life of luxury. It was exactly the sort of bushwa that inevitably attaches itself to a weird, foreign vagrant who spends a sizable portion of his day hollering at sparrows.

"The Hun ain't got no secret stash of gold, like they say," Pete sneered. "He ain't even German. He's Swedish or Viking or one o' them countries."

"They got gold in all of those countries," Kender pointed out.

"Then why don't he cash some of it in and get himself some new clothes or a decent meal?" I'd engaged in variations of this debate, with any number of people, pretty near my whole life.

"Because he's crazy. Shell shocked. He thinks we're still at war with Germany and that there's *boche* spies watching him, just waiting for him to tip his hand."

"And you think we'll be able find his stash of gold when all these German spies can't?" Pete asked.

"There aren't any spies, you sap. He just thinks

there are. And anyway we're Hungarian, and American, and that's worth a least a battalion of lousy kraut spies."

This proclamation very much appealed to our egos, so in a sort of patriotic fervor, we decided, then and there, to relieve the Hun of his gold, immediately.

Immediately being somewhat delayed by the time it took us to return to our various homes, collect impromptu weapons, regroup at Danny's Corner, and then walk all the way across town, over the River Bridge, and through the deserted rail yard.

By then my enthusiasm, at least, had cooled considerably. It didn't help that it was starting to get dark. Aside from broad daylight being, well, broad daylight, it had the advantage that the Hun was generally out and about by day, collecting trash and furthering his vendetta against the birds. I wasn't so afraid of slipping into his shed while he wasn't there, ransacking it a little. Even if there wasn't any gold – and I think we all knew that there wasn't – he might have some little money lying around that we could grab, or maybe something we could sell. But now, this late in the day, he might actually be there, and that could lead to a confrontation. And with me carrying an axe handle and Pete a hammer and Kender a pry bar, well, a confrontation might get messy.

"We oughta wait until tomorrow," I ventured.

"We already come all this way," Kender countered.

"I'm parched," Pete added.

Yeah, there was that. I was definitely in a state, and I found myself hoping that the Hun would maybe have a bottle of rotgut stashed in that shed of his, so I could settle the beast.

And then, too soon, there it was.

Run-down and isolated, like some fairy tale witch cottage, backlit by the sinking sun. An orange-red light, distinct from the fleeing daylight, danced and flickered within, visible through the gaps between the boards.

"Rhatz!" Pete frowned. "He's home!"

"Mind your fucking language," Kender whispered. "And keep it down!"

"What are we gonna do?" I asked Kender.

"Thinking. Thinking," he said.

"What is he doing in there?" I wondered aloud. "It looks like he's got a fire going."

"What if he's burning the gold?" Pete gasped.

"You really are dumb," Kender said. "He's probably trying not to freeze to death."

"It's hot as hell," I pointed out. This was true. It was the middle of August.

"It's different with old people," Kender soldiered on. "They're always cold." We were rapidly losing our focus and Kender knew it, so he made a decision. "Here's what we're gonna do. Dicky, you sneak up there and peep between the slats and see what he's up to. If he's sitting there tempering his knife collection or something, we ought to know about it. If everything's copacetic give us the thumbs up and we'll start raising hell and when he comes out here to confront us we'll keep him busy while you slip inside and grab whatever's worth grabbing. Got it?"

Pete and I nodded.

"Well get going then!" Kender exclaimed.

Keeping low, I crept up to the side of the shed, and peeped inside.

The Hun wasn't tempering knives. That would have been a lot less strange than what he actually was doing.

First off, he wasn't wearing any clothes. His long dirty hair and some blessedly convenient shadows concealed most of him, but I was still seeing some things I had no interest in seeing. He sat, tailor style, on the floor, hands raised, palms down, mumbling some gibberish under his breath. On the floor in front of him he'd painted this squiggly shape, and placed around the shape were six or seven sputtering candle stubs, the source of the light we'd seen. Even from where I was the place stank, like sweat and wet animal. *What the hell is he up to?* I wondered.

A hiss from behind redirected my attention. I turned my head and spied Kender, making a *Well???* gesture with his hands.

It was one of those moments, I suddenly realized, a sinking feeling in the pit my stomach. Right now, this very instant, was a sort of fork in the road, and I'd been blessed from above with this realization so that I might steer the proper course. And I almost did. I swear to anyone and everyone I almost did. But I peeked back through those slats one last time, just to get a last look at whatever it was the Hun was up to, and I saw it, there, on what passed for his mantle.

A bottle.

And that surely wasn't water in it.

I got the craving, bad. It hit me like judgment from above and my head exploded and my hands started shaking so hard that I was barely able to give Kender and Pete the thumbs up.

As promised, they started raising hell. Whooping and shouting and play sword fighting with their hammer and pry bar.

The Hun burst out his front door, such as it was. He hadn't even bothered to put trousers on, and his particulars was just swinging in the breeze, free as one of them birds he so despised.

"What you kids dooink here?! Get oon with you then!" he shouted at them. Me he didn't notice, planted against the side of his shed like I was.

"Go back to Germany, Hun!" Pete responded.

The Hun took a step toward them. I was shocked at how thin he was, underneath the ragged layers of tattered clothing he generally wore, even in the summer months. Nothing but skin and bones and hair, and I felt a pang of pity for him. He wasn't some romantic military deserter gone to seed, he was just a sick, crazy, dying old man.

"Who you calling hun, then? I'm no hun!" he railed

at the others.

"That's your name!" Kender needled him. "The Hun!"

"My name is Bjorn! I'll kill you both!" He took several rapid steps towards them and then froze.

We all did. Because Kender had discarded his hammer and produced, from underneath his shirt, a pistol.

"Where did you get that?" I heard Pete gasp.

"So you goots a gun. You think I'm afraid of your gun?" the Hun – Bjorn – scoffed.

"You'd better be," Kender said, his tone far less confidant then his words. "Dicky!" he hissed at me. "Get in there and get the stuff!"

Bjorn finally noticed me then.

"So three of you, huh? Three of you to rob Bjorn. Or is there more?"

"Quiet!" Kender ordered, gesturing with the pistol.

"You shoot me?" Bjorn said. "It would be a favor. Except of course it would not."

That would make much more sense to me later, to my eternal regret.

"Dicky! Sometime before sunrise, okay?"

Nodding, I ducked into the shed, grabbed the bottle first, unscrewed it, and took a long pull. It tasted like bilge water but it burned going down and I presumed that was good. I tippled it again, and once more, then recapped it and stuck it under my belt. Then I proceeded to search the place, but halfheartedly, suddenly wanting nothing to do with any of this, and feeling nothing but shame and pity for the Hun. Bjorn. I was so careful I didn't even topple over a single one of his stubby candles. Mismatched, they were barely even stubs, I realized, looking at them now. Clearly he'd fished them out of the trash. Several people's trash. For some reason that broke my heart.

"There's nothing here!" I called out to the others.

"'Noothink here', he says!" Bjorn laughed out loud.

"They rob the poorest man they can find and are surprised he has noothink! Stupid!"

"Mind your tongue, kraut," Kender warned him.

"Maybe I pull yours out, eh?" Bjorn pressed, advancing on Pete and Kender again. Pete took a step back but Kender didn't.

"I'm warning you," Kender said.

"And I'm warning you!" Bjorn countered, continuing to advance. "I eat little boys like you, and maybe your mother too, yes? Only because willpower I don't! You should thanking me, not sticking pistol at me!"

"Put the gun away," I said.

Bjorn started. He'd apparently forgotten about me, and now he re-positioned himself so that he could keep all three of us in sight.

"Get back in that hovel and find something we can spend, or sell, or drink," Kender ordered.

I didn't like being ordered around by Kender, and I told him so.

He told me what I could go and do, and who I should do it to.

The sun was well below the horizon now, but it wasn't quite full night. It was that weird, purple, in-between time, and my eyes were having trouble adjusting because it looked like ol' Bjorn was getting, well, bigger. Broader. More muscular. Not so sickly looking. Hairier, too, over his entire body, and that had to be my imagination because I *knew* he didn't look like that before. And I knew it wasn't just me imagining it, because Pete and Kender were staring at him too, half amazed and half befuddled. Bjorn doubled over then, seizing his stomach like he was in pain, and I swore I heard something inside him pop or snap or break. Like when you crack your knuckle bones, except way louder.

And that, for some reason, what the straw that broke Prawno's back, because he turned and bolted right out of there, like the hounds of Hell and every cop in the city besides was hot on his heels. Kender, I don't think he had the good sense to run, even, but he did back up a few steps. He held that damn pistol out at arm's length and he was shaking so bad I couldn't believe it hadn't already gone off.

"You-you stay back!" he choked.

Bjorn dropped to his hands and knees and made a funny sort of snuffling sound. And damn but I could swear that he was getting *bigger*.

"Kender!" I hissed. I sure didn't want him to pull that trigger. I knew in my bones that nothing good was gonna come of him pulling that trigger.

He pulled the trigger.

Bjorn screamed, sort of. More animal than human, the noise he made. And then Kender was running. And then Bjorn was lunging for me, because I was the only one not already running and anyway even before all this running had started I'd been the closest. He hit me with more force than I would'a thought possible and we went down, him on top, gibbering and snarling some foreign madness into my face, an impossible bulk weighing me down. I thought for sure I was a goner, even when I felt the sticky wet and knew that that fool bastard Kender had gone and done it. Bjorn the Hun was shot. He was dying.

"Yooooou!!!!" he growled in fury, and his nose in my face felt like a dog's nose and when I tried to push him off all I grabbed was fistfuls of hair. He made a funny sound in his throat and coughed up something warm and foul, right into my mouth, and I gagged and tried to spit it out but some of it went down.

And with that, he slid off me some, dead weight now, and I extracted myself from beneath him and I must've just been crazy with fear or something because he was, after all just a dirty, skinny, naked old man.

A dirty, skinny, naked old man who'd been shot, I remembered.

"I'm gonna get you some help!" I told him. "You

just hold on!"

"Too late for that," he grinned at me. It was an sly, knowing grin, and it gave me the heebie-jeebies. "It's yours now, boy, and in this curse let your weakness be your strength."

With that, he was gone.

Let your weakness be your strength.

As far as a curse laid on you by a dying man, that really didn't sound all that bad.

Famous last and all that, right?

I walked home, in the dark, finishing off the bottle I'd liberated from Bjorn the Hun's place. It was awful but it did the job, and by the time I was back on my home turf and had located Kender, I was sufficiently zozzled to ignore his pleas for mercy and knock the living tar out of him, right there in the street, and in front of some girlie he was trying to impress, yet. A bonus. That marked the dramatic end, so I presumed at the time, of our acquaintanceship.

No one ever came around asking about the Hun, and no one much commented on the fact that he didn't seem to be around anymore. Of course Prawno and I kept our mouths shut, and I can only presume Kender did too.

3

A couple of weeks slid away, hardly noticed, and the more things didn't change the more they stayed the same.

"One measly dime," Pete groused. "And that I found in the street." We were sitting at the counter at Frank's, quite pointedly not ordering anything. Frank was at the far end, working up the courage to tell us to leave.

"Why don't you ask your mum for some clothes money? Tell her you need a new suit to go job hunting." This angle had worked before, for both of us. You had to space the requests out though.

"She ain't got it. Didn't I tell you? The Phantom Burglar hit our house Sunday night!"

"Bastard," I commiserated. The Phantom Burglar, as he'd quickly come to be called, was the current scourge of our neighborhood. He'd victimized at least four families in just over a week. Oops, five now.

"He's shit. I'd like to get my hands on him."

The irony of our judging him was, of course, completely lost on us.

Just that very moment Daisy Duran sashayed through the door, and all other considerations and concerns vacated our noggins.

"Well," she declared, her voice dripping with poisonous honey, "if it ain't Dicky Illes and Prawno Pete, God's two answers to a question nobody asked."

"Daze," I nodded, maintaining my composure.

"Why don't you beat it?" Pete glowered, not maintaining his composure.

"Beat it? I just got here." She took the seat next to me. Daisy Duran, three years our senior, had embraced the fly-it-in-your-face flapper lifestyle with raw abandon, and she adored bad language. Bad as in poor, and bad as in vulgar. "Anyway Dicky wants me to stay, don't you Dicky?" she asked, tousling my hair. I did, and I told her so.

"Dicky thinks with his soup bone," Pete grumbled.

"I like a man with a big brain," Daisy said.

"So what brings you to our neck of the city?" I asked. Daisy was from the neighborhood, but she was much too pretty for it, and had finagled her way uptown months ago.

"I'm on a fact-finding mission, where *fact* equals *corn*."

"Bourbon specifically?" I asked. She nodded.

"The gentleman I'm currently pretending to be interested in favors it. Any leads?"

"We're so on the nut we're not even looking," I explained. Pete snorted in agreement.

"Poor little bunnies! There's a blow tomorrow

night, out my way, and word is they'll be swimming in it. Eighteen Brickard Street, in the Crown. You should crash." She slipped off the stool, "accidentally" hiking her dress up in the process, favoring us with a length of smooth, creamy thigh. She blushed – I swear she could do this on command – and not-so-quickly tugged the hem back down. "Caught ya lookin'!" she grinned. Then, like a beautiful tornado, she was gone.

"Whaddya think?" I asked Pete.

"Swell," Pete replied, noncommittally.

Tomorrow night came, as it will, and Pete still hadn't committed, so I went around Mousey's place to see if he wanted to crash Daisy's party with me. This was not merely an act of generous camaraderie. Mousey had a car – a beat-up Elgin Six – and Brickard Street was on the other side of the city.

There was an unseasonable chill in the air, and halfway across town I asked him if we could stop and put the top up.

"Nope," he told me. "I prefer to arrive in style and anyway we're almost there."

Brickard street turned out to be an undeveloped length of road culminating in a single house, situated at the furthest end. You could already hear the music, there were cars parked everywhere, half of them blocking the other half in even though there was plenty of room, and already there were people congregating out front, clearly tilted. But there was no one nearby to disturb, making it the perfect place for a raucous party.

Mousey parked relatively far away, to assure we wouldn't be blocked in.

"If John Jacob Jingleheimer Law *does* show up, I wanna be able to get out of here in a hurry," he explained. Good thinking.

We wove our way through the automobiles and the people, peeped someone taking donations at the door, and so wended our way around the side of the place so we could slip in through the back. This worked, and soon enough we were inside. The ground floor was almost entirely a single large, open space, unfurnished. A helical staircase sprouted from the center of the floor, leading upstairs. A few colored fellows were belting out some passable jazz from the far end of the front room, and lots of people were dancing. There was plenty of drink, and we helped ourselves.

"Sickly Dickly!" someone squealed, running up to us and seizing me from behind. It was too much to hope that it would be Daisy. No, it was Holly-Lynn Smith, one of my little sister's bothersome friends. Tiny, blue-eyed, and blonde, she was almost certainly on her way to being a prize beauty, but right now she was only fourteen.

"Fifteen!" she corrected me, irritably. "This is Dick," she explained to her two companions, one of whom I vaguely recognized as another sometime associate of my sister's. "He's Aggie Illes' older brother."

"Aggie's not here, is she?" I frowned. I didn't like the idea of my little sister drinking, especially at a mad blow like this.

"She. Is. Not," Holly-Lynn grinned, walking two fingers up my chest. She took a long pull from the hip flask she was carrying, then all three girls were struck with a fit of giggles and scampered off.

"I think that one likes you," Mousey grinned.

"Maybe in ten years," I said dismissively, inhaling my drink. God, but it hit the spot. I hadn't had a drop since... *that* night, when I'd grabbed that bottle from poor old Bjorn the Hun's place. And frankly the contents of that bottle hadn't done much for me, except fire me up enough to give that murderous snake Kender the beating he so richly deserved. Looking back, I'm not even sure it *was* booze. I found myself, not for the first time, or even the fiftieth, wondering if anyone had yet discovered the poor old man's body. Or was it still just laying there, slowly being worried away by animals and the elements? The thought depressed me, flooded me with guilt for the role I'd played in his tragic fate, and I decided that I very much needed another.

There was plenty – where had they managed to procure all this booze? – so I lifted an entire bottle of gin from the guy distributing drinks, tucked it under my arm, and climbed upstairs to see if I could find a secluded corner to put the better part of it away before someone noticed.

I'd polished off damn near half of it, by myself, standing on an upstairs balcony, when I heard something behind me. I turned to find Daisy bumbling through the bedroom door, but my smile died on the vine when I recognized Mousey as the one with his arms around her, saving her from a tumble.

"Oh, hey, old boy," he grinned. He had Daisy's lipstick on his cheek and collar. "Didn't know this room was occupied. Sorry."

"Come on, Ignatius!" Daisy insisted, dragging him away. That was Mousey's real name. A moment later they were gone. She hadn't even acknowledged my presence.

Well, like the great philosopher once said, fuck them. I decided to commit myself entirely to my drink.

It sizzled in my stomach, heavy and weird. No matter. It had been way too long, and I needed it. Time lost all meaning and I felt like I'd been sitting on that balcony all my life, drinking from that bottle, and would sit there for a hundred lifetimes more. Eventually someone else came into the room behind me and I wanted to tell them to let me be but my lips wouldn't work and was I really that smoked? Didn't seem possible, especially when I examined the bottle and saw that there was plenty left.

Now the intruder had taken a seat next to me and she plucked the bottle from my hand and I was okay with that because she had nice gams and now she was kicking her shoes off and she had nice feet too. I wanted to rub those feet. Kiss them. Marry them and take them home to dear old Ma.

"Vile," the girl attached to those feet said. "What is this?"

"Gin," I informed her. She took another long pull and passed it back to me and now her face finally came into focus.

"Holly-Lynn," I slurred in acknowledgment. "Where're your friends?"

"They're whores," she said. Clearly there had been some sort of incident. Probably involving a boy she liked. I could sympathize.

We sat there in silence for a while, passing the bottle back and forth.

"My mother won't let me cut my hair," Holly-Lynn finally lamented.

"You're hair looks nice long," I told her. It did.

"But it's not *stylish*. I want to be mod and stylish," she sighed.

My head was pounding, like my brain wanted to punch its way out of my skull and depart for places unknown, to live a life of its own without my constant interference and nonsense.

"Your mother let you wear that dress, but won't let you cut your hair?" I asked. Her dress was sinfully short. You could see her knees.

"I borrowed it from Ginny," she explained. "She's so lucky. Her parents don't care *what* she does."

I was getting dizzy, so I stretched out on my back, right there on the floor. Of course I didn't really have a choice, since there was no furniture.

I was looking up at Holly-Lynn now and I realized she was crying.

"You're pretty and nice," I told her. "Annoying, yeah, but pretty and nice. You don't *need* fancy clothes or a stylish haircut."

"You really mean that?" she asked, wiping a tear away.

"I do." I did.

She leaned over then and kissed me, a sweet, appreciative, brotherly thing. At least that's how it started out. But I kind of kissed her back, so she lingered, and suddenly it wasn't such a brotherly kiss anymore. Next thing I knew she was straddling me, and I heard the gin bottle we'd set aside topple over and break, and several intense minutes later I was fumbling into her, drunk but gentle, gentle, and her arms were around my neck and she was sighing in my ear, *"I always liked you..."*

Yeah, I kinda got that.

4

One of Holly-Lynn's shoes had gone missing.

"We probably kicked it over the side," I guessed.

"I'll go down and look for it," she said. She hesitated. "You'll wait for me, right?"

I nodded.

She continued to hesitate.

"Am I your girl now?" she finally asked. I could see

in her eyes that she expected me to say no.

Fifteen to my nineteen. All my friends would make fun of me, maybe even ostracize me. But I was starting to realize that my friends, well, they were mostly rotten human beings. I hadn't just been talking when I'd told Holly-Lynn she was nice. She *was* nice. Probably the nicest of my sister's little friends. My friends were layabouts and drunks, and let's not forget that one of them had just recently shot a guy. I was on a real bad trajectory. It was time for a change.

"Yeah," I said. "I want you to be my girl."

She squealed, and clung to me for a second, than ran off to find her shoe.

And I was glad to see her go, not because I actually wanted her to go, but because suddenly I felt like I was going to die. My headache was even worse, I felt like it was fire rather than blood running through my arteries and veins, and now my skin was starting to itch, bad, like the worst itch I'd ever experienced. Maybe I gotten some bad hooch. Dragging myself to the edge of the balcony and hanging over the balustrade, I stuck a finger down my throat and let it go, over the side, hoping nobody was down there, especially Holly-Lynn. That would be a fine how-to-do.

Regardless, upchucking didn't help, and as I was hanging there trying to decide if I should maybe find someone to take me to a doctor, my entire body went to hell.

First my back seized up, and let me tell you, this was, and remains, the single most painful thing I have ever experienced in my entire life. I prayed for death in those few moments, and I wasn't being hyperbolic. I fell to the floor, inexplicably too heavy to bear my own weight, then doubled over as I was stricken with agonizing stomach cramps. Every bone in my body felt as if it were snapping simultaneously, *everything* hurt, everything around me suddenly smelled much stronger and somehow worse, and now I could see that my arms weren't arms anymore: they were thick, powerful *legs*, sprouting thick black-brown hair even as I watched...

I can't go on. It's too much and anyway I think you get the idea. I'd turned, altered, changed... into a *bear*.

I had transformed into a *goddamned bear*.

Worse, I knew it. Understood. And worse yet, I couldn't do anything about it. The beast I had inexplicably, impossibly become clearly had its own agency, entirely separate from my own. I could only watch, through its eyes, as it lumbered around in a clumsy circle until it found its way inside, away from the confusing open-air confinement of the balcony. From somewhere beyond the space immediately in front of him, and just below, there was the most terrible racket going on, and a miasma of distressing, irritating smells besides. The bear did not like it. He didn't like any of it, at all.

There was a terrifying creaking, like something structural giving way, and the people who immediately looked to the sound were the first to see the gigantic bear attempting the stairs.

"I'm hallucinating, right?" a young man asked his date, and he wasn't wrong to ask, because not only should there not have been a bear attempting to navigate the spiral staircase from the second floor, but this particular bear looked nothing like any bear anyone present had ever seen before.

Massive it was, just shy of eight feet tall were it standing on its hind legs, its patchy fur a brown so dark it was almost black, eyes white and dead. Bone shown through in places, and rot, as if it represented the ghost of a bear rather than the living, breathing variety. But it most certainly had a physical presence, evidenced by the fact that its great bulk was already straining the stairs' anchors, eliciting a low groan of impending failure from them. The music stopped. The smart people were already bolting for the exits.

The bear was, of course, much too big to navigate the spiral and almost immediately got stuck, at which it panicked, thrashing and struggling against the sort-of cage it had trapped itself in. This was too much for the structural integrity of the stairs, and now they gave way, dramatically collapsing in a cascade of bear and screeching metal and chunks of ceiling. Even the stupid people were running now, trampling those who moved too slow, some of them literally diving out of windows. The bear, confused, enraged, and smarting from a bar of steel railing now embedded in one of his rear legs, waded in, roughly batting people aside with its gigantic paws. Some of these people didn't get back up.

Outside the chaos only increased, because everyone went for their vehicles but the automobiles were parked too close together, packed in too tight. A seemly endless cacophony of collisions as folks started up and tried to maneuver out of the morass, the bear galumphing right into the midst of it, swiping at people and vehicles, folks leaping out of blocked-in or stalled cars to flee on foot or grabbing hold of a car already in motion and trying to climb aboard. One fellow was leaping from hood to hood, trailed by angry shouts as his passage left huge dents in each. Another was desperately trying to crank his car only for the crank to break his arm when the engine caught and it got away from him.

And I, buried inside the beast, was witness to it all.

With no one currently in reach of his hungry claws he swung his massive head to and fro, as if searching for something.

He found it.

Mousey and Daisy, sprinting for Mousey's breezer.

Whether because the part of the bear that was me recognized them, or because I was still smarting some that Mouse had made the girl I'd come here to see, or maybe just because they were running the fastest and this got his hunting instincts riled up, Mr. Bear decided that *they* were the ones he wanted. Literally forcing his way between two parked cars, toppling one of them onto its side in the process, he gave chase.

"Oh my Goooooooooddd!" Daisy caterwauled as she realized they'd become the furious animal's chosen target. To Mousey's credit he made sure Daisy was safely inside before he started the engine, got the car pointed in the right direction, and dusted out of there, but all this gave the bear time to close the gap, and it was mere yards away by the time they really started to accelerate. Now, Mousey's Elgin can go pretty fast, but it takes time to achieve its full potential, and the bear was fast too, unnaturally fast. It caught up to

them with ease and took a wild swipe, connecting with one of the wheels, which shattered from the blow with the crackle of splintering wood. The car canted and swerved, Mousey fighting to retain control, Daisy screaming, the bear quickly regaining the ground it had lost when it paused to strike and so almost immediately on top of them. Mousey put the car into the ditch alongside the road because that was the quickest way to make it stop, then practically dragged Daily to safety even as the bear threw itself, bodily, onto the vehicle in a cacophony of groaning steel, splintering wood, breaking glass, and loud, irregular *pops*. Daisy quickly found her feet and thanklessly left Mousey behind, dashing across the vacant lot they'd found themselves in without looking back.

Mousey, meanwhile, tripped.

Overturning the car with frightening ease, a negligible obstacle to be effortlessly shunted aside, the bear quickly navigated the ditch and reached Mousey in seconds, rearing up on his hind legs over the young man even as the latter scrambled to regain his footing. I – I mean, the bear – let out a triumphant roar and...

There was a sudden, terrible smarting in his buttocks, like he'd been stung by the world's largest hornet.

More pops. That hadn't been something giving way inside the now-demolished Elgin. Someone had a gun, and was shooting at him.

Guns were dangerous, the bear understood, so without hesitation he dropped to all fours, turned, and ran, paralleling the road briefly, then crossing back over and fleeing into the fields beyond.

5

I woke up, naked, in the woods.

To be perfectly honest, it wasn't the first time. The morning-after headache was nothing unusual either, although this one was particularly bad.

I'd never been shot before, though, so that was new.

Bad liquor, that was my first thought. I'd gotten some especially bad stuff and hallucinated the whole thing.

Except that was bushwa, and I knew it.

It had happened, exactly as I (dimly) remembered it.

I'd turned into a bear. Run wild. Wrecked that party and maybe even killed some people.

And now I was lost, in the woods, with no clothes on and a bullet lodged in my rear end.

This latter was most surprising in that it didn't hurt as much as I would have thought, and I hadn't come to in a pool of my own blood. Actually, as far as I could tell, I wasn't bleeding at all. I reached back and touched the spot gingerly.

It was already healing over.

It was impossible.

No, not impossible. Supernatural. Like in those disintegrating penny books still stashed in Pa's old trunk. Demons, curses, werewolfs, and all of that. Except I guess I was a were*bear*.

It was the Hun, the Hun that had done it. He'd really and truly cursed me.

I broke down then and bawled, I'm not ashamed to admit it. Would this awful, inconceivable thing happen to me every time I...

Every time I what?

That stopped me in my mental tracks.

It'd been weeks since the incident with the Hun. Why was this only happening to me now? Did the curse take that long to fully take effect? That seemed kind of logically inefficient, I thought, for magic. Probably it was something I'd done that triggered it. My first thought, of course, was what had happened between me and Holly-Lynn. I surprised myself with how much I hoped that hadn't been it. God help me but it seemed I really was goofy for her.

Then, the curse might be random, just sneaking up on me at the most inopportune moments, which would be any moment, really, because when's an opportune moment to find yourself changing into a bloodthirsty terror-bear?

Of course there was also the dim chance that it would only happen the once. Lesson presumably learned, kid, now be off with you.

That seemed too much to hope for though.

Ma had about reached the end of her rope when I stumbled in early that evening, wrapped in a pilfered bed sheet tugged off a clothesline, dropped off by the smirking motorist who'd given me a ride, and she swore such oaths as I never thought I'd hear pass her lips. I was bedridden into the next day, from a vicious chill picked up during my misadventure, and the pain in my rear (which, truth be told, had rapidly diminished to almost nothing, though I swore I could still feel the bullet in there). Agnes delighted in my misery, although she was kind enough to bring me a newspaper reporting on the event, at my request.

"Bear Breaks Up Bacchanal!" exclaimed the headline. Other second-page news concerned a new postage stamp honoring Lindbergh, and the further depredations of the Phantom Burglar. Apparently the latter had been surprised in the course of his latest intrusion, and had threatened the victim with a pistol before escaping. He was described, to little useful end, as "a young man, successfully concealing his features behind a cloth mask".

"You were at that party, weren't you?" Agnes excitedly asked.

"I was," I confessed. "But don't tell Mother. She worries enough as it is."

"Did the bear bite you on the bottom while eating your clothes? Or were you already naked when it bit your bottom?"

"If you must know," I frowned, because I knew she would have it out of me before she'd leave me in peace, "I injured myself running away from it. Fell into a water-filled ditch, ruining my clothes, and, yes, landed square on my bottom."

This satisfied her, as it made me look foolish, and she temporarily let me be.

Sometime after noon Holly-Lynn came around, asking after Agnes as a pretense to see me. Ma let her in, and left not long after on business of her own, leaving we three alone. Holly-Lynn immediately covered my face with kisses, and then clung to me. Agnes was aghast.

"My brother?!" she asked incredulously.

"It's true love," I informed her, piling it on. My sister's face went a little green.

"We're going to be married!" Holly-Lynn added, and now my face was the one going green. At this, Agnes laughed so hard she nearly fell over.

"You two *are* a pair!" she smirked. "You deserve each other. I wish you a very miserable matrimony!"

Holly-Lynn stuck her tongue out at Agnes, then turned her attention back to me.

"I was afraid you'd been shot!" she exclaimed, peppering me with kisses again.

"Shot?!" Agnes gasped.

"There was a fellow with a pistol," Holly-Lynn explained, "I suppose he was trying to shoot the bear, but he was shooting every which way. I don't think he knew what he was doing."

"Was everyone at this mad bear party but me?" Agnes frowned.

"Don't tell Mother," I reminded her.

"Shot at... attacked by a bear... seduced by a girl of unusually ill repute... why shouldn't I tell Mother?" Agnes asked with a grin.

"Ill repute?" Holly-Lynn comically gasped, abandoning me to punch her friend in the shoulder.

I laughed along with them, but it was hollow laughter, and even later, when Agnes graciously left Holly-Lynn and I alone, I found myself distracted by a slowly coagulating sense of dread. What if it happened again, and I hurt Holly-Lynn? Or Agnes? Or Mother?

Tomorrow, I decided, at first light, I would return to the scene of Kender's despicable crime, to which I was unenthusiastically but inarguably an accessory, and see if I could learn just what it was Bjorn the late Hun had done to me.

6

I pointedly started out at dawn, despite a thoroughly sleepless night, utterly opposed at the thought of revisiting the place before the sky was bright and the sun high in it. Besides the clothes on my back I took only two things: my father's old suit-case, and a dollar which I had begged off Agnes (I had no idea where she'd gotten it), and to any curious onlookers I probably looked as if I were running away from home. I don't doubt that some of the neighbors in the two dozen or so shanties clustered around our own would have welcomed this.

It was nearly noon by the time I reached the rail yard. I paused a moment to survey the scene, but little had changed. The Hun's body was still there, already reduced to bones, and these spread out across a significant area. Scavengers, I presumed. I located his skull and as much of the rest as I could and gave him, well, not a *proper* burial, but the best that I could manage. I was forced the dig his grave into the dry, packed dirt with a flat of scrap steel I searched out, and I chastised myself for not bringing a shovel.

That done I said a little prayer over the man's final resting place and then let myself into his appropriated home, to see what I might find.

As it turned out, not much.

Filthy linens spread neatly across an old cot. A battered old travel trunk. Shelves lined with more scavenged candles. These were the whole and all of Bjorn the Hun's possessions in this world. And we'd thought to relieve him of his *gold*. I shook my head. Opening the trunk I discovered more linens, some foreign coins in a lidless jar, and...

A book.

And what a book it was. Bulky and unwieldy, bound in cracked black leather with tarnished brass fittings. It certainly *looked* like something a wizard might own, and record his diabolical spells in. In that I was disappointed, however, because the handwritten text inside more closely resembled the entries in a diary, and this written in an incomprehensible combination of English and a language I didn't recognize and peppered with clunky, unfamiliar words like *transmogrification* and *kallohonka*. I'd need a dictionary *and* a translator to make sense of it.

I returned the book to the trunk, sat down on the cot, and tried to sort it all out. What was it the old man had said? Let your weakness be your strength. What did that mean? Well, drink was my weakness, clearly. That and poor taste in friends. And I had been drinking when *it* had happened. I played with the dollar in my pocket. I would have to find out. I would have to positively identify the trigger before I hurt someone I cared about.

I stashed my suit-case behind Bjorn's shed and went off in search of booze.

It took me the better part of the morning and into the afternoon, because this wasn't a neighborhood I was intimately familiar with, but eventually someone directed me to a place where I was able to trade my dollar for four drinks. Not enough to put me down, by a long shot, but I polished them off in rapid succession and I was feeling pretty fine. I rushed back to the rail yard, already flushed with an unfamiliar heat, my skin red and itchy, my hands (and feet!) cramping painfully, like a man with arthritis.

So this was it, then.

I quickly undressed and stashed my clothes in my suit-case, and that back behind the shed. It was happening, I could feel it, a tingly agony building inside of me, more intense by the second. The bones in my face popped and I could *feel* my features changing, extending.

I screamed, and kept on screaming until the scream deteriorated into a snarl, not of agony, but of confusion and vague irritation. There was a small woods bordering the far end of the yard, another reason I'd chosen to do this thing here, and I – that is, the werebear – lumbered towards it, drawn by the tightly-packed, welcoming trees and a million distinct scents I hadn't noticed before. Deep in the creature's head I felt as if I were sinking, drowning in a sea of bright emptiness, and then, like a light winking out, everything that made me *me* was gone.

I have no memory whatsoever of what the werebear did while I was away. I surfaced hours later, a man again, bedded down amongst the trees not too very far from where I'd started.

7

It was late when I returned home, not that this was unusual.

What was unusual is that I found the front door of our cramped, narrow shanty wide open. I hesitated. Had someone come for me? The authorities perhaps? There was no logical reason to think so, but I'd spent the better part of the day as a *bear*, so logic was kind of out the window.

Hesitantly, I approached the door, stealing a glance in either direction, seeking, I suppose, some potential assistance. But the houses on either side were dark, their occupants asleep or absent.

A figure stepped out of the dark doorway, out of my *home*. A man.

"Hey!" I shouted and he started, clearly caught unawares, and then ran, clutching something to his bosom, bounding across the muddy slum-roads and disappearing into the night. The near-full moon revealed him as a young man, about my age, his features concealed behind a cloth mask.

Concealed, but not successfully. Because I knew those eyes.

I rushed inside, fearing the worst.

And finding it.

Agnes was sprawled on the floor, his first victim. Next to her was my mother, who'd apparently interrupted the deed. Both of them had been shot dead.

I fell to my knees and wept. I should have been there.

I should have been there.

"If you know who the Phantom Burglar is, you should tell the police," Holly-Lynn insisted for the hundredth time, gently clutching my hand. She meant well, but she didn't understand. We sat on the bank of the little river where this had all started, with me and Prawno and...

Kender.

"No," I said, also for the hundredth time. "But I need your help. I need you to tell all your little friends, everyone you know, that I know who he is, and that I *am* going to tell the police, unless he meets with me. Tell them to tell their friends, and them to tell theirs."

"What if...?" That was all. Apparently she couldn't bring herself to finish the thought.

"He won't," I promised her.

"And after you settle this, we'll run away from here and get married?" she asked.

"Yes," I lied.

"We could go to Chicago," she said without enthusiasm, like she knew I was lying.

Agnes and Ma were dead because of the rotten company I'd kept, and now I was hurting the girl I think maybe I loved. If anyone deserved to be cursed, probably it was me. But did it have to be so on the nose? Did I really need to transform into an actual, literal monster... when I already was one?

"Tell everybody," I repeated.

8

There's a bank of fog rolling in off the water now, and as it settles in around me like a grey, damp hug somehow I know I'm gonna make it. I chose the pier for our little rendezvous just to make sure there wouldn't be anyone else around to interrupt, or accidentally get hurt. I insisted on three in the morning for the same reason. Kender, of course, will presume that this is all, quite accidentally, to *his* advantage.

He'll have his pistol with him, I imagine.

But I have the werebear.

I have no doubt whatsoever that he'll come. I know him. He'll come and, not immediately finding me waiting, he'll nervously stalk around in ever-growing circles, shouting my name, promises, threats, his words dripping with false bravado. Then, when he's finally shouted out and thinking maybe it was all a ruse, I'll take a long, invigorating drink – my last – and point the bear at him.

So long, Kender.

And after?

During the long walk here I'd almost convinced myself that I'd find a way to stow onto one of those big ships anchored in the harbor, let it carry me away to parts unknown. Start over. But really I know better. I can't resist the siren song of the drink, not forever. Sooner or later I'll give in. That makes me a danger to everyone around me, friend, foe, and stranger alike, and there really is only one viable solution. I know it's a mortal sin – the worst – but if it's done under extenuating circumstances, for the greater good, maybe He takes that under consideration? The turn my luck's taken, though, I'm guessing not. Probably I should say my goodbyes now.

So goodbye, Aggie.
Goodbye, Ma.
Goodbye, Holly-Lynn.
Goodbye.

Johnny Cocksure and His Giant Fucking Robot

"John... Cocksure?" the student volunteer at the door asked hesitantly. They always asked hesitantly, even if they knew you from another class. Even if you were best friends outside of school. "He's needed in the principal's office," the girl explained.

Johnny groaned inwardly, even as some wag snickered and stage-whispered *"Busted!"* Why now? Why today? There was a pep rally next period. He loved sports but – for obvious, eternally frustrating reasons – couldn't play. Was it too much to ask that he at least be allowed to enjoy them vicariously? Just once in his fucking life?

With the weight of the world apparently on his shoulders he slouched out of the room, Mr. Bergin's admonishment to get the reading assignment from someone else in class later flapping like a tattered flag behind him.

When he reached the office, the secretary handed him the landline receiver. "Your mother," she explained. "Something about a dental appointment?"

"Johnny!" gasped the overwrought male voice on the other end. "This is Number A!" Of course it was. "Lord Crown Spider has unleashed the Kanga-Rabbit on Moscow! We need the Big Robot!"

Moscow? Didn't Russia have its own giant robot to deal with things like this within its own borders? Why was it always the Brigade of Light's responsibility? Why was it always *his* responsibility?

"She said she'll pick you up out front," the secretary informed him gratuitously as he handed back the phone. He sighed heavily. "I hate the dentist too," she commiserated, trying to be nice.

Not bothering to acknowledge this, Johnny marched out of the office, up the hall, out the front doors of the school, and around to the west side of the building, where hopefully only a few dozen students and staff would notice when the *gigantic fucking robot* showed up and landed in the overflow parking lot. As opposed to the entire school seeing it land out front, as if that made a difference. Extracting his phone from his pocket, he opened the secret app, not so brilliantly disguised as a common but unpopular social media application, and tapped the icon.

Then he waited, fuming.

He was fifteen now. Almost an adult. And he was goddamned sick of this Big Robot business. So far, this year alone, he'd been called away from two sporting events, three assemblies, and one dance. And then there was that kicking party where he'd been offered beer by a couple of seniors but couldn't partake, because something might happen and after all one couldn't be piloting a giant robot all over creation, drunk.

The whoosh of boiling, superheated air as, seconds later, the Big Robot arrived, all the way from its secret hanger on the dark side of the moon, in violation of several laws of physics. "Big Robot, pick me up," Johnny ordered dully into his phone. The great mech landed, kicking up dust for blocks around, then bent down and gently collected its human component, depositing him in its chest cavity, which then sealed itself automatically. From the control module within, Johnny, and only Johnny, was in complete control the massive mechanical.

"Quickly, Johnny!" Number A's voice blared from

the interior communications system. "There's no time to lose!"

There was never any time to lose. Never time for *anything*.

"To the skies," Johnny ordered with zero enthusiasm. Big Robot lifted off, kicking up more debris, and nearly toppling over one of the cars in the teachers' parking lot. Its passenger-side windows were both shattered in the process, and Johnny absently hoped that the car didn't belong to one of the teachers he especially liked.

Now they were airborne, Johnny ordering the Big Robot to Moscow, not bothering to clarify further or even glance at his phone to pass the time because they were there in no time at all, which should have been impossible but the impossible was the name of the game when it came to the Brigade of Light, the Big Robot, Lord Spider, and all the goddamned rest of it.

Lots of farm country unfurling beneath them, Johnny noted, and then there it was, Moscow, and smack dab in the middle of the city flailed the enemy mech, a nonsensical zoological amalgamation that appeared to be half kangaroo, half rabbit. *Gee, I wonder what this one's gimmick is?* Johnny asked himself sarcastically even as it leapt impossibly high into the air, seized the Big Robot and dragged it back down to earth. Naturally they landed right on top of the biggest, most ostentatious building around, crashing straight through it, destroying it utterly. "Thank God that building was already safely evacuated!" Number A informed Johnny via radio, which, quite frankly, sounded like the bullshit that it probably was. They always said that.

The Kanga-Rabbit mech was bounding up and down on the prone figure of Big Robot now, even this simple action a vulgar violation of physics to anyone who was paying any real attention. This wasn't doing the Big Robot any serious damage but it was preventing him from rising so that he could get on with ending this thing. It was all so tiresome. If everything was safely evacuated, couldn't they just drop a nuke on this fucker and call it a day?

"Johnny Cocksure!" cackled a wearyingly familiar voice. Lord Crown Spider, sporting, as usual, that ridiculous hat, appeared on Johnny's monitor, literally rubbing his hands together with glee. "This time I have you, and the whole Brigade of Light! Soon the Earth shall be mine!"

If I drank a shot every time this goony asshole said the Earth would be his, Johnny reflected, I'd have died of blood alcohol poisoning years ago. He was so beyond sick of this endless, tiresome cycle. Lord Crown Spider attacks a random city with a mech. Johnny and the Big Robot hand him his ass. He tries to escape and comically stumbles into a swimming pool or falls down a flight of stairs with a bucket on his head. Brigade of Light agents nab him. Seconds later he escapes. Wash, rinse, repeat.

I'm never going to have a normal life, Johnny realized. I can already see it: there I am, in the back seat of my first car, about to lose my virginity, finally, when the Big Robot lands right next to us, tipping the car over and sending my date screaming into the night, because a giant mechanical wildebeest is trashing Akron, Ohio or something. I can't take it any more. Do I really still want to be dealing with this nonsense when I'm forty???

The Kanga-Rabbit was at the apex of its current impossible bound when Johnny ordered the supine Big Robot to quickly, unexpectedly sit up. The other mech landed squarely on Big Robot's head, breaking *something* so that its noggin now canted dramatically to one side. Gasps from the agents watching the battle from afar, heard through the robot's radio, but Johnny confidently ignored them. Instead, he concentrated on ordering Big Robot to seize the Kanga-Rabbit's left leg and then slam it repeatedly to the earth, bringing down half the street as he resolutely bashed the enemy mech to pieces. *Good thing all those buildings were safely evacuated, I guess,* he told himself cynically.

Cheers over the radio. "Johnny! You did it! Big Robot did it!"

Big Robot continued to lift the functionless, demolished mech into the air and slam it to the ground. Again. Again. Again.

"Johnny? We're good. Uh, Johnny?"

Again. Again. A dozen times more than necessary. He didn't stop until there was nothing left of the thing. Ripping what remained of his mechanical opponent's head off, he tore it in twain and extracted the tiny, struggling figure inside.

Lord Crown Spider.

"Curse you, Johnny!" Spider shouted, struggling comically in the Big Robot's careful grasp. "Curse you, and Big Robot! I'll get you both, next time! You and the entire Brigade of Light! Someday, the Earth *will* be mine!"

"Nice work, Johnny!" Number A congratulated him over the radio, though there was a nervous hesitation shading his praise. "Light agents will collect Lord Spider immediately so that he can be tried for this latest crime!"

"No," Johnny said.

"Come again?" Number A said.

Slowly, gently, Big Robot placed Lord Crown Spider on the ground. Then, even as the villainous would-be conqueror stared in confusion, Johnny ordered the robot's great fist back and sent it plummeting down with the power of a million locomotives, instantly reducing Lord Crown Spider to a gooey paste. And he didn't stop there. Again and again the robot's massive fist came down, pounding the smear on the ground that had once been Lord Crown Spider over and over and over, the heat and pressure produced unimaginable, until there was nothing left of the villain but a fine mist wafting around the bottom of a six-foot depression in the ground, even this quickly scattered by the wind.

"Final...episode," Johnny announced. He'd wanted it to sound ice cold and kind of badass, but it came out more like a sob.

"Jesus H. Christ," Number A opined. "I think that kid is in serious need of some therapy."

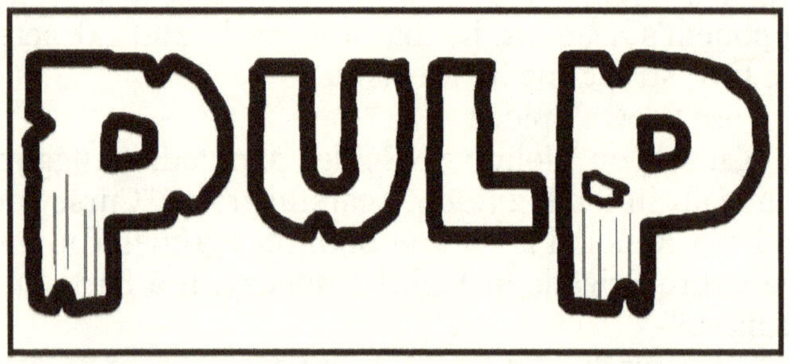

IN OUR NEXT INSTALLMENT:

Headless Jack, Part 2
Vic Campion: Adventurer
Crash! Baxter
The Tower of Death
Quentin and the Desk

Pulp: Adventure. Watch for it.

ABOUT THE AUTHOR

Brad D. Sibbersen has written fantastic fiction of all stripes, including horror, science fiction, gothic romance, comedic high fantasy, fae western, post-steampunk space opera, Victorian gaslamp vampire action, and retro-pulp new adult sci-fi/horror time travel adventure. In his spare time he reads weird books, listens to gothic rock, and watches obscure movies on defunct formats. He won't shut up about Hallowe'en or bunnies, and if there was such a thing as a Hallowe'en Bunny he would probably lose his mind. He loves you and he's so glad you bought this book.